Bribery

Dead of Night Series, Volume 2

Lexy Timms

Published by Dark Shadow Publishing, 2022.

This is a work of fiction. Similarities to real people, places, or events are entirely coincidental.

BRIBERY

First edition. December 21, 2022.

Written by Lexy Timms.

Bribery

THE DEAD OF NIGHT BOOK 2

USA TODAY BESTSELLING AUTHOR

LEXY TIMMS

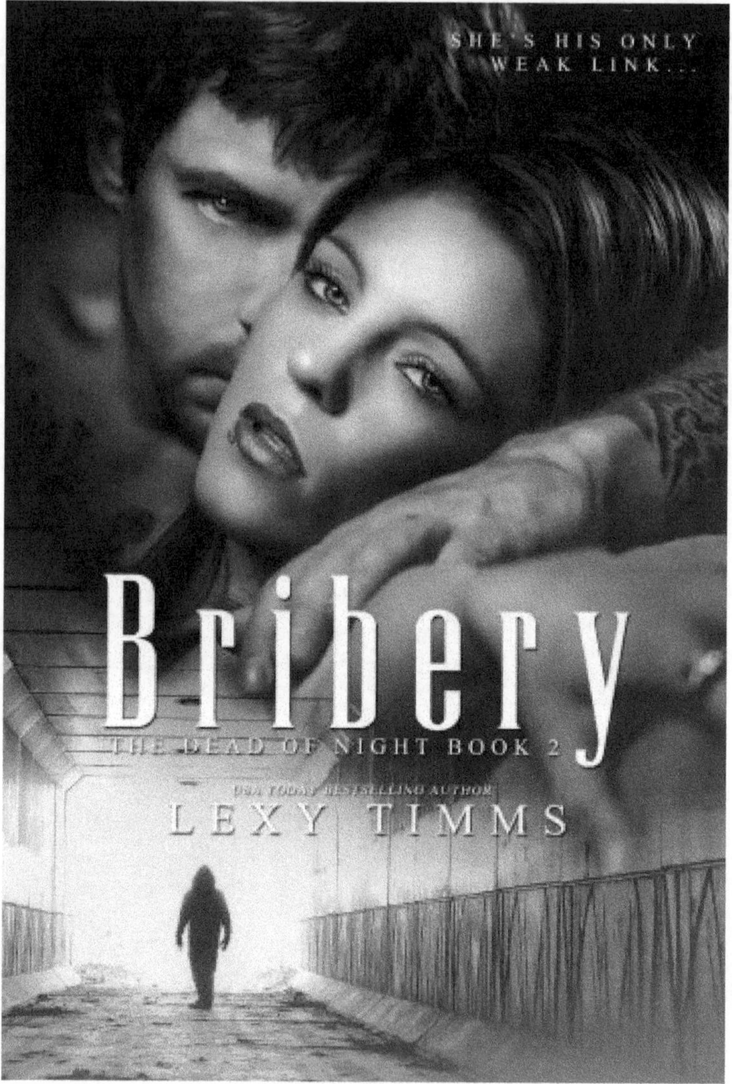
SHE'S HIS ONLY
WEAK LINK...
Bribery
THE DEAD OF NIGHT BOOK 2
USA TODAY BESTSELLING AUTHOR
LEXY TIMMS

Bribery

Dead of Night Series #2

Cover by: Book Cover by Design[1]

1. http://bookcoverbydesign.co.uk/

The Dead of Night Series

Abduction
Bribery
Corruption

The Heat of Night Series

Depravity
Scandal
Disgrace

Find Lexy Timms:

LEXY TIMMS NEWSLETTER:

https://www.lexytimms.com/newsletter

Lexy Timms Facebook Page:

https://www.facebook.com/SavingForever

Lexy Timms Website:

http://www.lexytimms.com

Want to read more...
For **FREE**?
Sign up for Lexy Timms' newsletter
And she'll send you updates on new releases, ARC copies of books
and a whole lotta fun!
Sign up for news and updates!
https://www.lexytimms.com/newsletter

BRIBERY Blurb

HONESTY STANDS AT THE gate and knocks, and bribery enters in...

Amber has finally dumped her cheating ex and realized I'm the man for her. From here on out, it's easy sailing, right?

But my father's health issues force me to spend more time on the family business than with her, and soon, tensions begin to rise in our new relationship. When the chance for a trip to Italy arises, I want to sweep her off her feet and show her just how serious I am.

When an unexpected attack pulls me away from her, though, she finds comfort in the last person I would expect...

She's his only weak link...

Briber
Bribery

Chapter One

Josh

"NOW, MARIO, COME ON," my mother scolded my father for what felt like the millionth time that night. "You have to eat healthy if you're going to recover from this."

"I'm fine," he muttered, reaching for his mask so he could take a huff from the oxygen tank behind him. I glanced over at Tommy, who raised his eyebrows at me incredulously. This had been turning into something of a routine since Dad got back from the hospital.

His heart attack had been serious, serious enough that he'd wound up in there for two whole weeks before they were comfortable letting him back into the house again. Mom had gone all-out, making sure the place was totally decked and ready for his return—every piece of medical equipment, every non-slip mat in the bathroom, everything was in place, and he had care takers coming in twice a day to check on him.

Though I knew he must have hated that part. If there was one thing my father prided himself on, it was not needing to rely on anyone other than himself. Right now, though, he was stuck having to play along with what the rest of the family wanted from him, and he knew it was for his own good.

Right now, we were trying to have a nice family dinner, a chance for us to sit down together and spend some quality time as a whole. But my mom had served up a carefully-prepared salad to my father instead of her usual decadent *penne alla vodka,* and I knew it was getting to him. He was basically refusing to eat, and I could tell it was driving my mother up the damn wall.

"Please, Mario," she begged him, and he reached out for his fork with a scowl on his face and took a bite of his salad. Much as he was pissed at all of this, he knew better than to annoy my mother. She had been so on edge after what had happened to him, it would take her the best part of the year to come down from it.

It had been tough for all of us, really, seeing him in such a state. We all knew he was getting older, of course, and the way he lived his life, a health problem was always going to happen eventually. But even still, the shock of it had been enough to take us all by surprise, and since then, we'd all come together to really focus on getting him back on his feet.

I couldn't fight the feeling, though I knew it was irrational, that some of this had been my fault. I should have been more accommodating instead of pushing him the way that I had, forcing him to take me in hand in ways I knew he didn't like. The best I could do—the best I had done—was to take care of everything I could and make sure he came out the other side unscathed. I had been working closely with Tommy, doing everything I could to make sure I looked out for him and held up my end of the bargain, even though it had been damn near exhausting to me.

"You know, none of us are going to eat until you do, Dad," Tommy reminded him with a grin on his face.

"If we wait for these two to stop arguing about it, we'll be here all night," I added, and everyone laughed. It felt as though we had been more of a family since all of this had happened, though I wished it could have come at any other time, in any other way.

Anyway. I was here now, and this was the best I could do. I wasn't going to let him down again. I had sworn myself to that, and I planned to keep it that way.

"You want more wine, Amber?" Tommy asked, turning to the woman beside me. Amber smiled and shook her head, pointing to her still half-full glass.

"I'm all good," she assured him. I smiled at her and squeezed her hand underneath the table. She had been amazing these last couple of weeks, and I wasn't sure I would have gotten through them without her. Her sweetness, her kindness and patience with me, even when things were hard, had been a lifeline when I needed it most.

And I knew it couldn't have been easy for her. Much as she kept telling me she didn't even care about the end of her engagement, the way it had all gone down was messy. Her best friend sleeping with the man she intended to marry? How exactly had Kimmy and Aaron planned to pull that off? I had no idea how they had gotten away with it for so long, but then, when the two people closest to her were in on the same lie, maybe it had been easier to handle than I had imagined.

She had been by my side through all of this, even though she hadn't even met any of my family. She didn't question it, helping out in any way she could, stepping up to go with me to the hospital even when she had been studying late for her exams. She was in the midst of one of the most stressful times of her life, but you would have never known it from the way she was acting.

My mother loved her. My mother, to be honest, probably just loved the fact I was with someone who wasn't a total bimbo for a change. I hadn't brought home many women because it usually didn't take me long to work out that the ones who wanted into my kind of world were usually doing it for the money and not much else. They often didn't have a whole lot going on between the ears, and I would soon grow bored of them.

But Amber? Amber was different. She was smart, funny, sharp—she would talk back to me, never afraid to tell me when I was being cocky or acting like an asshole. I loved that side of her. She must have been working so hard to hold it down when she was with her ex, because now that it was out, she seemed ready to tease me any chance she got.

Tommy seemed pretty impressed by her, too, which told me everything I needed to know. I knew my brother would want things a certain way when it came to the new people we allowed into the family, he would want someone he could trust, and even though she was training to be a lawyer, he still seemed to have time for her.

Of course, we had kept it vague about the truth of what we really did for a living. No way was I going to just spill something like that to her when we had barely been together a couple of weeks. I would have to take it slow, make sure she didn't get too many ideas about the kind of person I was before I had a chance to prove otherwise. She was coming into this pretty much blind, and I didn't intend to scare her away by being too honest about what was happening.

We were still having too much fun to want to break the fantasy. I wasn't going to let anything get in the way of us now, not when we were starting to have so much damn fun together. I loved being with her, loved spending time with her, loved getting to know her. And hey, even though the circumstances hadn't been perfect, at least she'd met my family, right?

Finally, Dad started to eat, and the rest of us tucked in, too. Amber was usually pretty quiet during these dinners, but beneath the table, she would tease my thigh with her fingers, reminding me just what we were going to do when we had the chance.

By the time the meal was finished, Mom was already fussing around Dad again, and he looked even more irritated than he had before. I poured myself another drink, and as I went to sit back down, I noticed Dad looking at me.

"What is it?" I asked him, concerned that I had managed to do or say something wrong. The last thing I needed was to cause him more stress, given the current state he was in.

"I'm just...very impressed with you, son," he replied finally. "It's good to see you stepping up and doing right by this family."

It felt like a dig, but I knew he was genuinely trying to offer me a compliment right now. My father had never had an easy time telling us the good stuff, even if I wished sometimes he would have been a little better at pulling it off.

"Thanks, Dad," I replied, nodding.

"To see you pulling your weight around here, just like Tommy's been doing—you'll be on his level soon enough, if you keep it up."

I tensed. Okay, that was harder to take as a compliment. But the way he was looking at me, I could tell he meant it. He didn't have anything good to say about me that didn't reflect on my brother, too, and I guessed I should have expected it. Much as I wished he could take me on my own merits instead of just brushing me off like this, it was his way of trying to tell me he was proud of me.

"He's doing well on his own, Dad," Tommy cut in quickly. He was probably worried that I would freak out if Dad said something like that to me, and I guessed he had a point. I hadn't always been the best about taking my father's attempts at compliments, but I didn't want to stir the pot. He was trying to tell me he was proud of me, and after so long feeling as though I was letting him down, it was good to hear.

"No, I get it," I replied. "Thanks, Dad."

The rest of the evening went by without much drama, even as Mom and Dad bickered about the best way to deal with his heart now he was back home. She insisted on getting him off for an early night, leaving Tommy, Amber, and me to spend the rest of the evening together.

I could tell Amber was a little intimidated by Tommy. I got it—we were so alike to look at, but there was nothing similar about who we were as people. I put an arm around her waist, and she leaned into me, as though grateful for my presence, glad I wasn't going anywhere.

He poured us all a drink, handing Amber her glass first, as he had long been taught to do by our mother. If there was one thing she valued above all else—even my father's heart health right now—it was manners.

"You think he's starting to do better?" I asked, referring to our father. Tommy shrugged.

"I think he's starting to accept he'll need more of our help than he thought he would," he replied. "Not sure what that means for Mom, though. I don't know how she's going to be able to keep up with everything he needs now that he's back here again."

"She'll be able to cope," I replied. "You know how she is. She always takes things in hand."

"You're right," he sighed in agreement, pushing a hand through his hair. I knew this had been particularly hard on him given how close he was to Dad. He was used to working closely alongside him, and having to step up and take control of everything himself must have been tough. I could see the dark smudges beneath his eyes, giveaways of the nights he had been staying up trying to deal with all of this.

Amber sipped her drink and looked between the two of us. I wondered how fast her mind was running right now. She must have still had so many questions about what was going on here, what business we were actually in. I had told her the pawn shop was the main focus, which wasn't exactly untrue, but I was sure she was on the brink of figuring it out at any moment.

"You want to go out?" I suggested. "I could use a chance to blow off some steam."

"You think that's a good idea?" Tommy asked, looking a little concerned. "If Dad needs us—"

"Dad's going to be fine," I told him, reaching out to place a firm hand on his shoulder. "And you're not going to feel any better sitting around here worrying about him. Mom's going to take care of him; haven't you been listening to her tonight? She's not going to let anything happen."

He inhaled deeply and closed his eyes, nodding. He knew I was right, even if he was having a hard time admitting to it. He never took it easy when he had to deal with stuff like this. Even though we were the same age, I got the feeling he often felt like the more mature one, the one who had to do more to keep things running.

"You're right," he agreed, and he downed the rest of his drink. "Let's get out of here. I could use a break."

Chapter Two

Amber

JOSH HAD HIS ARM DRAPED along the back of the booth, his fingers tracing out a shape against my neck. The softness of his touch was enough to make my whole body shudder with delight, and I wondered how much longer I was going to be able to keep myself together.

He and Tommy were talking shop—something about where they were planning to meet with a buyer, I figured for something from the pawn shop. I knew there was more to their line of business than Tommy was willing to tell me, but I didn't want to push any more than I already had. If he wanted to tell me, I would know about it, and I was done pushing my luck for now.

It had been a crazy couple of weeks, since the confrontation at my old place with Aaron. I mean, it was technically still my home now, but I hadn't been back there much, too worried about what I would feel if I was there alone. Besides, it had been way more fun to hang out at Josh's place, plus it was closer to the law department, too.

Helping him out with his dad had been hard, but I figured it was the universe's way of putting me through the wringer and making sure I could handle something as big as this. It had been less than a month since I had ended things with Josh, but I didn't have it in me to miss him at all. If anything, I was glad he was gone, and I hoped he was sorting his shit out so someone else didn't have to come in and do it for him.

Someone like Kimmy. I almost felt a little bad for her, but then I remembered what she had done, and I didn't have it in me to actually care so much about how she was handling it. She was the one who had been sneaking around behind my back this whole time, fucking my fiancé. No wonder she had gone out of her way to make sure I thought I was crazy for even considering that he might be cheating. She needed to keep me in the dark so I wouldn't second-guess what was happening there.

I wished I could go back in time and tell her I saw right through that, but it wouldn't have changed anything. I knew I was better off without either of them, and I was glad I didn't have to worry too much about what was happening when I wasn't looking anymore.

Of course, I missed the hell out of Kimmy. That was the worst part of all of this for me, by far, knowing my best friend had been so eager and quick to make a move on my fiancé when I wasn't looking. I had never taken her for the kind of girl who would act like that, but I guessed you never really knew anyone. Maybe you could never really hope to, either, and it was better to just let it go how it was going to go instead of controlling it.

Besides, I had more important things to think about right now. My exams were coming up in a week, and I refused to let all the time I had spent working for this go to waste. They had come at the worst possible time, but I figured there was going to be a lot of this over the course of my career. Lawyer hours were hardly known as the most convenient.

Either way, it was nice to be out with Tommy and Josh and forgetting about all of it for a while. We were in the VIP section of a small, exclusive club not far from his family's place. There was a huge line at the door when we arrived, but we were ushered right by that, past the red rope cutting us off from the rest of the clientele, to a special booth at the back where they served us top-shelf champagne apparently without charge.

I knew Josh couldn't have this many ins all over the city by chance. There had to be something going on here I didn't see, but I didn't want to know, not tonight, at least. It was easier to drink, to flirt, to have fun with the guy I was dating. We were still in that honeymoon period, unable to keep our hands off each other, and I didn't want it to end.

I hadn't really mentioned him to anyone yet. The only thing most people in my life knew was that I wasn't wearing an engagement ring anymore, and I didn't want to talk about it. Whatever had happened between Aaron and me, I felt as though I needed to keep it to myself. I didn't want to share more than I needed to, especially when I was having so much fun in this new relationship.

It had been so long since I'd felt the first flush of love like this, and it was making it hard to think straight. I knew I was going to need to pull myself together sooner or later, but I was dizzy over him, unable to focus on anyone or anything but the way he made me feel. His touch, his love, his want for me, it all made me feel like I was hardly touching the ground most of the time, my feet trailing a few inches above the earth whenever he slid his arm around my waist.

Tommy got up to go to the bathroom, leaving Josh and me alone for a moment. He turned to me, a smile on his face, and I felt desire start to rise up inside of me. It was so hard keeping my hands off him when we were around his family, but the more time that passed, the better I was getting at controlling myself.

"Let's dance," he told me, rising to his feet and grabbing my hand. I had never been much of a dancer before I met him, but every time we had gone out together, he usually ended up swaying with me on the dancefloor. I had noticed a few women shooting me annoyed looks when they saw us together, as though they wanted him for themselves.

I still didn't know a huge amount about his reputation in this city, but I got the feeling that his impact on the women here was pretty sizeable. He already knew about my dating history, he had been there when my last relationship had gone to shit, and it was strange to think that he already had so much knowledge about that part of my life when I seemed to have none of his.

I pushed it down as he led me out to the dancefloor, sliding his arms around my waist and pulling me close once we were in the throng of people. I smiled and sighed with relief as he nestled his head into my neck, his breath on my skin.

It was easy to forget about everything when we were together this way, and I didn't want it to end. I didn't want to have to face down the real world if I could help it, to think about what happened when reality started nudging in to our lives. When he touched me and pulled me in close, I couldn't think of anything but how much I wanted him. How much I wished the two of us were somewhere a little more private.

His hands slid down to my hips, and he pulled me in closer, holding me there right against his body as though he could sense the need in me in that moment. I looked into his eyes, seeing his desire for me, and felt another warm rush of heat pulse into my veins. I had never felt anything like this for anyone before, this crazy need that seemed to get the better of me no matter how hard I tried to control it.

He moved his lips to mine, brushing them gently against my skin, and a shiver rushed down my spine. I couldn't control myself right now; I couldn't make sense of how I was feeling or what I wanted next. He gripped me a little tighter, pulling me on to him as though he couldn't get enough. The alcohol and the music and the want mixed within me to create something I couldn't control, something I wouldn't have wanted to, even if I could.

His tongue slipped into my mouth, and my knees started to go weak. How was I supposed to last the rest of the night with his brother if he was going to insist on making me feel this damn *good?* I needed some kind of relief, something to take the edge off, or I wasn't going to be able to focus.

When he pulled back from me, I cupped his head in my hand to hold him still and lowered my lips to his ear.

"We need to get somewhere private," I told him, my voice low, trying not to attract the attention of anyone around us. I knew plenty would be trying to overhear what we were saying to one another, but I needed it to stay just between us. A secret we could share.

He grinned as he pulled away from me, the look on his face telling me he understood just what I was getting at. He kissed me again, harder this time, pressing himself against me so I could feel the stirring of his cock beneath his pants before he grabbed my hand once more and led me back toward the VIP bathrooms.

Chapter Three

Josh

AS SOON AS WE WERE inside, I pulled her into my arms, thrust my hand into her hair, and kissed her.

I knew we might get caught here, but it was hard to give a damn when my desire for her was getting in the way of all my rational thought. I didn't want anything, anything but her—her body, her kiss, her hands all over me.

She moaned against my mouth as I turned her around to face the small mirror, putting her hand on the sink for balance. I wanted to look at her while I fucked her, see the expression on her face as I moved deep inside of her and filled her with my seed.

I pushed her short dress up over her hips and groped at her gorgeously bare ass—the only thing between me and her right now was a pair of black panties, and I pressed my hard-on into her so she could feel how much I wanted her.

"Please, will you just fuck me?" she whined, wiggling her butt back and forth against me as though she didn't know how to control herself. I loved it when she got like this, so desperate for me to fuck her she couldn't think of anything but having me inside. I hadn't taken her for the kind of girl who would have been into something like this, but we were learning a whole lot about each other right now, and every little detail had worked for me so far.

I tore off her panties, tossing them aside, and then took my cock in my hand and aimed it at her soaked pussy. She looked back over her shoulder at me, and the needy expression on her face sent another surge of need through me. I planted my cock into her and thrust deep, filling her to the brim in one motion.

"Oh, my..." She moaned, hanging on to the sink and letting her body slide back against mine. It was as though she had been waiting for this all day, holding out with everything she had to let me fuck her. Her hand on my leg beneath the table at dinner suddenly seemed a lot more pointed now that we were doing this.

The thought of her needing me for so long before she could take what she wanted sent another shockwave of arousal through me. Everything this woman did turned me on. I watched her face in the mirror, her jaw tense and her eyes closed as she focused on the pleasure I was sending pulsing through her body. She knew how much I wanted her, how crazy she made me, and I could see that she felt just the same way right now. After so long of both of us holding back and trying to deny how we felt about each other, to finally be able to dive into it was a relief bigger than I could have expected.

I could hear the music still pounding outside as I slid deeper into her, bending her over a little farther so I could slide into her harder and faster. She moaned again, her breath starting to take on the ragged edge I had learned was a sign she was close to coming.

I wanted to see her come. I wanted to see her give in entirely to the pleasure I was giving her right now. I gripped on to her hips to pull her back against me, driving myself so deep inside her I could feel her beginning to clench as her orgasm drew close. She lifted her gaze and met mine in the mirror, and the moment she did, I watched as she finally reached her release.

"Oh, fuck," she groaned, biting down hard on her lip to try to contain the passion. Though the music was loud out there, I was sure at least a couple of people wandering by would be able to hear us doing this. Not that I cared. Let them—I liked the thought of someone being jealous about us in here, taking what we needed from each other.

I pushed in deep one last time and felt my cock twitch as my own orgasm rushed through me, my toes curling in my shoes as I filled her with my seed. I couldn't take my eyes off her reaction in the mirror, the way she responded to me as though she had been craving this for as long as she could remember.

I slowly pulled myself out again, and she gasped as she tried to catch her breath. I loved seeing her like this, unable to think about anything but how good it was for us to be together. She would come back down to Earth soon enough, but for now, she was still up in the stratosphere.

"Where are my panties?" she mumbled as she looked around the bathroom trying to find them. I winced.

"Sorry, think I'm going to need to get you a new pair," I offered, and she shook her head at me as she pulled her dress down as far as it would go.

"If I get thrown out for indecent exposure tonight, I'm holding you personally responsible," she warned me as she slipped my hand into mine. I grinned. As though I was even going to let anyone else look at her right now.

I felt like I could have taken on the world. With a woman like her on my arm, nothing else came close to mattering. Anyone could have said anything to me, and it would have bounced right off. Hell, I'd even managed to take my father's attempts at a compliment well tonight, which I wasn't sure I would have pulled off if she hadn't been around...

As soon as I pushed the door open, though, I was confronted by a sight I wasn't exactly thrilled to see. It took me a moment to recognize him, but when I did, I felt my heart sink.

Damon Daniels. The son of an old colleague of my father's. His dad had gotten a little too greedy and fucked up beyond what my own father could fix for him. Damon had ended up doing some time over it, but it looked like he was out on the streets again now—and on top of that, as though he had a serious bone to pick with me.

"Damon," I greeted him, trying my best to ignore the glower on his face. I wasn't going to let him spook me. No, I knew I had the run of this place if I wanted it, and I wasn't going to let some two-bit criminal wannabe get in the way of that.

"Josh," he replied, blocking my path as I tried to brush past him and go back to where we had been sitting with Tommy. My brother had noticed something was up, his head popping up over the booth to keep an eye on the situation. I would bet he had clocked Damon before this but had hoped it wasn't going to turn into anything serious.

I put my arm around Amber. I could feel how tense she was as she clung on to me. She'd never had to deal with something like this before, and I would be damned if I let this be the night she encountered one of the unsavory characters I happened to be associated with.

"Can we get back to our seats?" I asked him calmly. He might have just had a couple of drinks and would think better of this when he figured out what a mess he was making. He clearly thought he was calling the shots here, but I wasn't going to let him make a fool of me in front of Amber.

"I need to talk to you," he growled. "Not once—not *once* after my father hit the skids did you or your family do anything to help..."

"We did a lot to help, Damon," I replied as diplomatically as I could. I could feel my fist curling, ready to swing at him if I needed to. One of his guys was standing just behind him, staring at me, unblinking. He was trying to scare me. But I'd dealt with enough shitheads like this in my time to know there was no point giving in to whatever they were trying to pull off.

"But your father was so determined to run his own business into the ground there wasn't a lot we could do to stop him," I continued. Might not have been the nicest way to put it, but this man needed a reality check. He'd been away for long enough, stewing on what had happened, he had lost sight of the real problem here—and it had nothing to do with us, that was for sure.

"Don't you talk about my father like that," he demanded, and he jammed his face up close to mine. I felt Amber being pulled away from me and realized one of his fucking goons was getting her out of there.

"Hey, don't you fucking touch her!" I yelled, and I went to grab Amber, but she had already wriggled herself loose, and Tommy was heading over to make sure the situation didn't get too crazy.

Damon swung for me, so drunk he could barely aim in the right direction, and then I landed one on him, sending him sprawling to the ground. He grunted loudly as the crowd around him made space for him to crash to the floor, and Tommy squared up against the guy who had grabbed Amber. After a few moments, the man opposing Tommy seemed to think better of it and dropped his head down to slink away again.

"Don't come near me again," I spat at Damon. "And don't even *think* about looking in her direction. You understand me?"

He didn't look at me, wiping a streak of blood from his lip. I leaned down to grab his collar, forcing him to look up and face me.

"I said, do you understand me, Damon?"

Finally, and after a long pause, he nodded. He didn't want to concede the point to me, but he knew he would be fucked if he tried to fight this. I dropped him again, letting him fall back to the ground with a thud and instantly turned to see if Amber was all right.

I took her by the shoulders gently, looking to see if they had hurt her. If they had so much as laid a finger on her, I would kill them, right then and there. I didn't even have to think about it.

Luckily for them, though, she looked relatively unharmed, though I could see from the distant, slightly vacant expression on her face that she was shocked by what had just happened.

"Are you okay?" I asked her, and she didn't answer for a long moment. She must have been stunned at the two of us going from hooking up like that to being confronted by someone who had beef with my family. She hadn't been exposed to anything as bluntly as this before, and I hated that it had come on a night like tonight.

"Amber," I murmured again, and she finally looked up at me, as though registering I was there in front of her.

"Yeah, yeah, I'm fine," she replied, shaking her head. "Just a little...surprised, that's all. I'm okay. They hardly even touched me."

Hardly even. It wasn't good enough. I needed to make sure nobody got that close to her again. If she was going to be coming out with me, then I had to prove to her she had nothing to fear, that I was totally capable of protecting her. Just because nothing had gotten more serious tonight didn't mean it never would.

"Come on, I need another drink," she told me, grabbing my hand and pulling me close. I was going to be glued to her side for the rest of the night. If anyone so much as looked at her in a way I didn't like, they were going to have to answer to me. I wasn't going to let anyone put her in danger. She had already been through enough.

And I needed to prove I was a safe place for her. Not a place she was going to land in even more trouble. She had been through enough as it was, and I refused to allow her to get pulled into anything else that would have hurt her. She deserved someone who took care of her, someone who knew they would be able to look out for her no matter what. If there was anything, anything at all I could do to keep her safe, I would do it.

But before we could get back to the bar, we were being escorted over to the door. They didn't want any more trouble tonight, they told us, and, despite my protestations, they weren't going to take no for an answer. I sighed as we reached the door, holding Amber close to make sure she knew I wasn't going to let anything happen to her.

"You okay?" I asked, and she nodded.

"I'm good," she replied, though she still seemed a little shaken. I supposed after something like that, it was to be expected. She had probably never had to face off against someone like that, had to deal with the reminder that things weren't as smooth or as safe as they had seemed so far.

"Let's get out of here," I told her, and Tommy nodded from the other side of the door. We didn't need a place like this to have fun. I would take her back to my house and remind her just what a good time we could have together.

When we weren't being bothered by the scum of the Earth who seemed to want to make problems for us, anyway.

Chapter Four

Amber

AS I LAY IN BED NEXT to him, I stared at the ceiling, thinking about what had happened at the club.

I was still a little shaken up by it, but I didn't want Tommy to know that. I was sure he would have been beating himself up enough about what had happened, and I didn't need him to start going any deeper into his guilt and anger.

Who was that guy, the one who had confronted us? He had seemed genuinely pissed, and I wondered if I would have taken his side if I had known the truth.

I didn't know what his family was involved in, not really. I had picked up little snatches of it here and there, and the confrontation he'd had with Aaron at my old place should have told me everything I needed to know, but it was hard for me to take it all seriously. He was so kind with me, so gentle and generous, I didn't want to believe he had anything like that in him.

I saw a side of him I supposed he didn't make a point of showing to the rest of the world. He had to be strong to everyone else, had to make sure he was totally in control and commanding of everything that happened around here. His father seemed to need him now more than ever—though it was hard to believe Josh had ever been absent from their family business, given how frail his dad seemed now.

He was sleeping next to me, in his bed back in his apartment, and he seemed restless. I wondered if he was spooked by what had happened. It was, after all, the first time someone had come up to the two of us when we were out with the intent of causing trouble. I had no doubt there were plenty of people all over the city who had a problem with him, but we'd been lucky enough not to run into any of them yet.

How many more were waiting for the chance to get in his way and cause him problems? I didn't even want to think. The enormity of it was starting to sink in now, and I knew we couldn't just duck away from the consequences because we were together now. His real life was still out there, waiting for him, but now, he had me to think of. I was going to put so much more stress on him, and I didn't want to be the cause of his problems.

But I was sure I would be from here on out. People were going to work out we were together, and when they did, they would use me as a way to get to him. I was sure of it. Especially given what I was doing for a living, or would be, when I graduated.

I had been trying not to think about the impact my new relationship was going to have on my career going forward, but it was hard to pretend that I didn't see what a mess it could be. It would be way too easy for people to use it to discredit me—if I was involved with someone like him, how could I be expected to uphold the law in my day job?

I chewed on my lip as I looked over at him. Honestly, despite it all, right now, it felt worth it. I had no idea how long this would last, but the way he treated me, the way he held me, the way he looked at me as though I was the most precious thing in the world, it was enough to make me forget.

I was falling for him, and I knew I didn't stand a chance at pulling myself back from the brink right now. When he looked at me, I could feel myself starting to give in, all my better judgment just vanishing from my mind as I did my very best not to let myself get distracted by him. He was gorgeous, sexy, smart, funny—he was protective of me in a way nobody had been before, and, after being someone's second choice for so long, I had to admit, it was kind of a turn-on.

Aaron had never given a damn about me, at least not since he had started the affair with Kimmy. The moment he had fucked her, he had basically admitted to himself he didn't give a fuck about me or what happened to me. I wished I could have called him out on it face to face, screamed at him and told him what I thought of him, but he was already gone. Whatever he was doing, it had nothing to do with me, and I was happy to leave him and Kimmy to whatever bullshit they were getting up to now.

Josh had stood up for me. The way he reacted when they laid hands on me, it was like he couldn't control himself, like he wanted nothing more than to beat the shit out of them right then and there. If his brother hadn't been there to cool the situation off, he might have.

I had never been with a guy who would have fought for me before. I had never thought I would like it, to be honest, but there was a part of me that really did enjoy knowing he would have gone to bat for me if he needed to. Had anyone ever cared about me so much before? When he'd purchased me the bracelet, he'd told me it was a promise, a reminder of how much I deserved. Was this what he had been thinking about? Me deserving a protector? Someone who was really willing to fight for me?

I turned over and laid my hand on his chest, and he took it in his sleep. I could see a sheen of sweat on his brow, and he seemed to be having some sort of bad dream. I wished I could reach inside his head and lift it out, make it so he could rest easy after what he had done for me tonight, but I had no idea what he was thinking of.

He must have been through some serious shit. I had seen marks on his back, scars that looked new, and I hadn't asked him about them. Had he been in a fight? I couldn't imagine he would let someone do that to him without fighting back. He was too strong to sit back and let himself get hurt. Unless there was something else going on I didn't know about.

I wished I could ask him, but I didn't want to push for too much, not now. He had already been through hell as it was, with what had happened with his father. He was still reeling from it, though I was sure he would have denied it. I couldn't imagine what a shock it was to see your dad in that kind of state, especially given the power his father normally seemed to have over the family.

"No," he mumbled in his sleep. I smoothed his hair back from his face, and he twitched, jerking away from me. I was sure he was deep in some nightmare right now. He talked in his sleep sometimes, but it was hard to make out the details of what he was saying. He would swallow his words, even his subconscious doing its best to keep them under wraps.

"I love her," he murmured, twisting his head away from me. I gazed at him. Was he talking about me? I had no idea. I didn't want to assume I had managed to get that far inside his head yet, to be the subject of him talking in his sleep, but we were getting closer and closer. I knew he was in mine, whether I wanted to admit it or not.

I laid myself over his chest, gazing up at him, and he wrapped his arms around me tightly, as though he was making sure I didn't go anywhere. I closed my eyes and squeezed him close. I needed him to know I wasn't going anywhere. This relationship might not have been the most conventional, but it was the one I wanted right now. After so long being fucked around by someone who couldn't have given less of a damn about me, to have someone who would have done anything to keep me safe was a powerful thing, and I didn't want to lose out on it.

I listened to the slightly labored rise and fall of his breath and propped myself up on his chest so I could look at him. Whatever he was going through, he didn't deserve to be so afraid. He had protected me tonight. He and his brother had come to my rescue in a matter of seconds, which was more than I could say for anyone else in my life. I needed him. I needed him, and I wasn't going to go anywhere right now.

I patted his brow dry again and snuggled back down in bed next to him. I was going to get him through this night, no matter what was going on inside his head. He deserved to have someone here who would help him, especially after the way he had stepped up for me.

I closed my eyes and tried to slow down my breathing. It was all going to be okay. Just because tonight hadn't exactly gone how we'd planned didn't mean we were losing anything. We were still doing this. We were still together, the way we had been before, and I wasn't going to change a thing about it.

Right now, all I wanted was to get some sleep and forget about everything that had happened at the club. It was already behind us. And with any luck, it wasn't going to happen again anytime soon.

Though, as I lay there beside him, I wondered if I was telling myself a lie. Could I really believe it? I could try.

I needed to try.

Chapter Five

Josh

AS I WAITED OUTSIDE the dressing room, I noticed one of the girls at the counter glancing over at me. I paid her no attention. Plenty of people in this city knew who I was, and most of them didn't want to talk about it if they could avoid it.

Besides, this was about Amber, not me. I had taken her out shopping for her graduation dress, and we had been out for hours now trying to track down the right one. I knew she had planned to do this with her ex-best-friend, and when she had mentioned going out to do it alone, I'd known at once I wasn't going to let that happen.

I wanted to treat her, especially after what had happened the night before. I was still a little shaken about being confronted like that in the club, with Amber by my side. I had wanted to keep her as far from everything as I could, but it was getting harder and harder to handle as I tried to push down the doubt and worry in my mind. How many more times were we going to be interrupted the same way? How many people out there would want to cause trouble when they saw me out and about?

She was beyond nervous about finding the right dress. I knew this was a big deal for her, and I was so proud of her for passing her final exams. She had been working her ass off the whole time I'd known her, and now she was stepping out into the real world to begin a profession she'd been working toward for years. Of course, that profession happened to be upholding the law, which I wasn't sure would fit with my particular career, but I could deal with it. Sometimes, you had to take things as they came, even when they didn't seem to make much sense. I would find a way to make all of this work.

My family knew about what she did, of course, and I was certain Tommy had his doubts. He had been kind enough to her so far, though, and I hoped that meant he was able to see she wasn't any threat to us. She had clearly seen enough to make her wonder, but she wasn't letting anyone else see it. She wasn't going to report us or anything, and I knew she understood she would have to look the other way a little when it came to my family business. I wasn't going to ask her to get involved with anything, lie for us or something, and I hoped it would be enough to give her conscience the freedom she needed.

She stepped out of the changing room in a banana-yellow dress, and I could tell from the look on her face she didn't like it. I was biased—I thought she looked good in everything—but this wasn't the one.

"I feel like a banana split," she muttered as she peered over to the mirror and frowned at herself.

"Yeah, it's not quite right," I agreed, and she sighed and shook her head.

"Sorry to keep you out for so long," she apologized. "I didn't mean to waste your whole day like this."

"You're not wasting my day," I assured her immediately, getting to my feet to give her a kiss. "Come on, let's find another one..."

One of the assistants came over with another small selection for her to try on, and she vanished behind the curtain again. I was itching to pull it back and slide in there with her, but I knew I would be overstepping. This was important to her, and she didn't want me getting all handsy.

I had noticed the assistants hovering around us a little more than with everyone else, and I figured someone had spotted me and ordered them to take the best care of us possible. I wasn't complaining. I wanted

Amber to have the best experience she could, especially as this was going so differently than how she had imagined.

I hoped I never ran into that Kimmy girl. I knew I'd have plenty to say to her if I did. How could she betray her best friend like that? How could she just turn on her? It made me sick to think about it. Yeah, I had done plenty of shitty stuff over the course of my life, but I had never screwed over someone close to me.

I would never have pulled something like that. I might have had my issues, but I knew how important it was to keep the people you cared about close. Stabbing them in the back would have consequences for the rest of your life. Things would never chill out again. Everyone else would look at you out of the corner of their eye, convinced you were going to fuck them over the first chance you got.

Finally, Amber pulled back the curtain again and struck a pose in her new dress. This one was black, with a long skirt, a deep slit that seemed to run practically all the way to her waist, and a corseted top that pushed her breasts up into the most gorgeous cleavage. I looked her up and down, hardly able to contain my lust for her.

"What do you think?" she asked, but I could tell from the look on her face she was already pretty sure how I was reacting to it. I shook my head slowly, taking her in, wondering if this gorgeous woman could really be mine.

"I think it's perfect," I murmured as I stepped toward her, sliding a hand around her waist. "But maybe not for graduation."

"I was thinking a post-graduation dinner, maybe?" she suggested, biting her lip playfully. Oh, her mind was exactly where mine was right now, and the thought of how much she wanted me sent a surge of desire through my system. If I could have grabbed her and snuck off with her to fool around right then and there, I would have, but I knew I needed to restrain myself. We were in public, and we had already tried to work off our desires the night before.

"Yeah, exactly," I replied. "Let me get it for you. Along with the dress you want for the graduation."

She widened her eyes at me. "You don't have to—"

"I know I don't," I replied, cutting her off before she could go any further. "But I want to. Is that okay?"

She beamed at me. She knew there was no point trying to get me to drop something once I had it in my head, and I was intent on spoiling her today. She deserved it, after how hard she had worked. And if it meant I got to see her in that criminally hot dress again, it was as much a gift for me as it was for her.

She went through a few more dresses, but eventually, she came out in a red number that looked perfect on her. It was hot, but not the kind that would distract from the rest of the ceremony. I could see her now, hair tied back, pair of heels, looking sexy as all hell, with me in the audience knowing I was the one who got to take her home.

"What do you think?" she asked. "I like it. I think this is the one..."

As my gaze trailed up and down her body, I noticed she was wearing the bracelet I had purchased for her. I had seen it on her a few times, but I wondered if she kept it on always and I just didn't notice. I had first seen it on her again when I had gone to her place to shake down Aaron, as though she had finally realized she was worth more than what he was giving her. Just like I had told her.

"I think it looks perfect," I agreed. I slid my hand down to her wrist, fondling the bracelet for a moment. "Looks good with this, too."

She smiled and then looked back up at me.

"I've been wearing it this whole time, you know," she murmured. "I didn't want to take it off. Ever since what happened with Aaron, it's just...it's reminded me of what you're willing to do for me."

"Anything, baby," I replied, as I pulled her in for a kiss. "Anything. You know that."

I planted a kiss on her lips right there in the middle of the store, sure we were getting some hard looks from the staff around us. I couldn't have cared less. Sometimes, I just couldn't keep my hands off her, and I didn't want to pretend for a second longer I could.

She sighed as I pulled back, gazing at me like there was so much she wanted to say she didn't even know where to start. She didn't need to say anything at all. I knew what was going through her mind—the same thing going through mine.

"I feel so lucky to have you," I murmured to her. "You have no idea, Amber."

"Oh, I think I'm starting to work it out," she replied, smiling playfully. I laughed, and then my phone buzzed in my pocket. I checked who was calling and saw it was Tommy.

"Here, take my card and get those dresses," I told her, handing her my wallet. "I need to talk to my brother. I'll be back in a second, okay?"

"Sure," she replied, but I saw the flash of concern spreading over her face when I mentioned Tommy. She was starting to catch on to what went on behind the scenes with my family, and I was certain she didn't like it.

I didn't want her to worry. This day was about her, and I wasn't going to let anything get in the way of it. She deserved a chance to just relax and have some fun, and whatever Tommy wanted from me, I was sure I could handle it without causing trouble for her.

"Hey," I greeted him as I answered the phone. "What's going on? Is everything okay?"

"Where are you right now?" he asked.

"Downtown. We're shopping for clothes for Amber's graduation," I told him, unable to keep the hint of pride out of my voice. I couldn't believe I was dating a woman like her, a woman with her skills, confidence, and passion. I had never imagined I would ever get with a girl with her kind of brains, but here I was, getting ready to head off to graduation.

"You need to head down to the gallery," he told me. "Laurence. You need to talk to him. We both do."

"I'm busy right now," I told him as firmly as I could, but I knew he wouldn't have been calling unless it was something serious. My brother didn't tend to ask for much from me unless he knew he needed it, and I wasn't going to be able to find a way out of this one.

"You need to make the time," he replied. "Drop Amber off at home."

I bristled. I wasn't leaving her like that. I wanted to see her in that dress again, maybe see her out of it, too. I wasn't going to dump her back at my place and hope for the best.

"I'll see you there in ten," I told him, not bothering to respond to the part about getting rid of Amber before I went there. Maybe it would be good for her to see a little more of what I did.

She emerged from the store, smiling wide, and handed me back my wallet. I took it and tucked it away as I told her what we were going to do.

"I'm going to call us a cab, we'll be done at the gallery in a few minutes," I explained to her. "That okay with you?"

She hesitated for a moment before replying, as though she wasn't even sure she wanted to go along with this. I knew how she felt. It must have been a lot for her, to deal with the reality of my work out of nowhere. But it would do her good to see what I was up to when she wasn't around, I was sure of it.

"It's okay with me," she told me finally, and I planted a kiss on her cheek and went to hail down a car. I didn't know what Laurence had managed to do this time, but I figured he was going to need my help to get through it. I wasn't going to let him get away with whatever he thought he could pull off.

And maybe I would get another piece for my apartment, too. Because if he had pissed my family off this badly, he was going to need to do whatever he could to make amends.

Chapter Six

Amber

AS THE CAR PULLED UP outside the art gallery, I felt a fizz of fear in my stomach. What the hell was I doing here? I was certain Tommy wouldn't have wanted me tagging along to this shake-down, or whatever it was, but I was way too hooked on Josh to turn down a chance to be with him.

I hooked the bag with my dresses in it over one shoulder as he opened the car door for me to step out. My heart was beating fast as I saw Tommy standing outside the gallery, a grim expression on his face. When his eyes slid over to me, he had a hard time hiding his irritation. He grabbed Josh by the arm and pulled him aside as soon as we were out of the car.

"I thought I told you not to bring her," he muttered, clearly intending for me not to hear him. I glanced away from them, pretending I couldn't make out a word they were saying.

"She's here now," Josh replied bluntly. "Come on, let's get this over with. I have other plans for today."

We made our way into the small art gallery, and I busied myself looking at some of the paintings on the walls around me as Tommy and Josh vanished into the back. It was quiet in there, but I could hear the voices of the twins and whoever it was they had come here to confront through the wall.

What were they doing at an art gallery? I hadn't realized how many people in this city seemed to rely on families like Josh's to get by. I would never have imagined in a million years that Aaron would have been involved with them, but he had been, and now here I was, standing at this quaint little modern art gallery while my boyfriend was next door trying to get the money he was owed out of the owner.

At least, I was pretty sure that was what was happening right now. I hadn't asked Josh too many questions on the way over here, and I was sure he didn't want me to delve too deeply into what was going on. If he wanted to share it with me, he would have. Maybe I was better off not knowing.

The work here was lovely. The paintings on the walls were all from the same artist, deep golds and shimmering reds gleaming in the low light of the gallery. I wondered if the person who had created them had any idea they were at the center of some messy shake-down by Josh and Tommy next door.

Tommy had been pissed I was here. I could tell that much. Why had Josh brought me, if he had known his brother was going to be mad? Maybe this was some kind of test to see if I could keep my mouth shut. I wasn't going to tell anyone what had been going on between us, but I wasn't sure if Josh really believed it yet.

He had been lavishing me with attention, with gifts and kindness, and maybe he wanted to make certain he wasn't throwing all of that at the wrong woman. I had no intention of turning it around on him, but I could see why he might have had his doubts about me. We had only been together for a few weeks; maybe he had been hurt before by someone who had had their doubts about what he did.

I couldn't play stupid about it forever. I was sure I was going to hit a point where I had to ask myself some serious questions about the man I was with, but right now, I was enjoying this all too much to look too closely and cause too many problems. I loved being with him. I really did. It was so exciting, in a way nothing in my life ever had been before. Unexpected, thrilling, always something new coming at me. How could I turn this down, even if I should have?

I didn't know how he was going to handle being at my graduation next week. I mean, what if someone knew who he was? The chances of him being able to slide under the radar seemed tiny. I would be looking at everyone there, wondering if any of them had involvement with Josh and his family. What they thought of him. If they lived in the same terror of him as Aaron had, while he had been hiding it.

My stomach twisted at the thought. I wasn't sure if I could take it. It was almost impossible to reconcile the image I had of Josh with the one the rest of the world had of him. I mean, how was it that someone so tender, so loving, so sweet with me, could be so frightening to others? I had seen the way the guy at the bar had confronted him, it was clear he had caused some major problems in his life. What if he did the same to me...?

I pushed the thought angrily down at the back of my mind. I wasn't going to even entertain it. He hadn't given me a single reason to be worried about something of that nature. He had been nothing but kind and caring toward me, even before we had been together, offering me a place to stay if I needed to get out of things with Aaron. He had been good to me. I wasn't going to forget it.

I heard raised voices and quickly headed back down toward the door. I didn't want to have to hear all of that shit. I knew it didn't have anything to do with me. Josh just hadn't wanted our day to be over yet, which was the only reason I was here.

Suddenly, quiet came from the room, and I figured it must have been over, whatever it was. I breathed a sigh of relief. I wanted to get out of here. I needed to put some space between myself and this kind of knowledge about what had happened between Josh and this Laurence dude. I didn't want to get involved.

Josh came striding out with a determined look on his face, as though he had achieved just what he intended to. I almost wanted to ask what had gone down, but I figured it was better for me not to know.

If he wanted to tell me, he would, and there was no way I was going to get involved if he wanted me to stay out of it.

Tommy followed behind, but the guy they had been speaking to hadn't. What had happened to him? Was he okay? I felt a stab of guilt, knowing I was letting something like this happen, but I managed to stamp it down inside of me. It wasn't my fault, it wasn't my problem. Whatever that guy had been up to, whatever he had gotten himself involved with, it had nothing to do with me. Maybe he deserved it, like Aaron—maybe he deserved to be confronted like this and made to face up to his problems. I didn't want to know a thing about it.

Josh slipped his arm around my waist like he always did and smiled at me as though nothing at all had actually happened. I managed to return it, even though I was sure it was a little shaky.

"I love the pieces here," I remarked, gesturing to the walls around me.

"You should pick one for me," he told me. I was a little surprised—I hadn't thought he was that into art. I had seen a few pieces at his place, but I had figured his family had gifted them to him or something.

"You like this stuff?" I asked, and he nodded, casting his gaze to the wall. Tommy brushed past us and walked right on out, already pulling his phone out of his pocket. Who knew what he had to take care of next, but I wasn't going to ask.

"Yeah, I think Laurence works with some great artists," he replied. "I picked up a piece from him a couple of months ago, actually. Haven't had a chance to get it hung up, but it's nice."

I cast my eye over some of the paintings in front of me, trying to figure out which one would be a good fit for him. At the end of the row, a small piece caught my eye. It was mostly deep brown and gold, but it was splashed through with this beautiful, vibrant blue that reminded me of his eyes.

I took his hand and led him over to get a closer look. It was an abstract piece, but it had this peaceful aura to it. I liked that. I could use a little peace in my life lately, and I was sure Josh felt the same way.

"What about this one?" I asked, and he paused for a moment while he eyed it, taking it in. For a moment, I thought he was going to say it was hideous and he didn't want it anywhere near him. But then he smiled and nodded.

"I love it," he agreed. "I know exactly where to put it, too."

The man they had been talking to sloped out of his room, and Josh waved him over.

"I want this one," he told me. "When can you get it to me?"

"Uh, sure," the man replied. He didn't look physically hurt, at least from what I could see, which was a relief. Josh nodded and squeezed me.

"Thank you," he remarked. "I love it. See anything here you'd like?"

I shook my head. I kind of just wanted to get out of there, put as much distance between myself and this whole situation as I could. I knew Josh was just trying to keep me included, but I didn't know how much I wanted to be included in something like this. Maybe it would have been easier not knowing.

The man vanished once more, and Josh strolled over to the door with me at his side. He seemed utterly unbothered by what had happened in there. How had he managed to get used to this? I wished I could ask him what was going on in his head right now, but I wasn't sure I really wanted to know the answer to that. He was doing fine, and that was all that mattered.

Chapter Seven

Josh

AFTER DROPPING AMBER off at my place, I headed over to see my father. I knew he would want a run-down on what had happened with Laurence, and I wanted to be the one to tell him.

It had gone well, I was pretty sure of that. We had gotten the money from him. In fact, he had handed it over the moment we walked through the door, and he didn't even flinch when I told him I wanted to get my hands on a new one of his paintings. I wouldn't be surprised if it was waiting for me in gift wrap when I got home.

I smirked at the thought, glad I had gone along with Tommy. I knew he was bringing me with him to make a point about how I needed to do more to help out with the family, but it was a relief to know I could take Amber without her freaking out. A part of me was testing her, seeing how far we could go before she stopped in her tracks and told me she didn't want any part of this.

I was starting to feel like she would hit that point eventually. She was green in all of this, so brand-new it almost hurt, and I wondered when it was going to be too much for her. She wouldn't have admitted it, but this was far out of the realm of what I knew she was used to. There would come a time when she had seen too much.

But it hadn't come today. She had kissed me as she climbed out of the car and told me to come back soon, and I didn't intend on leaving her waiting.

She was more or less living at my place now, even though she still had the house she'd lived in with her ex. I had asked her why she didn't want to go back, and she told me it was just too full of memories for her to handle right now. I didn't blame her. I could only imagine what it had been like to find out her fiancé was not just cheating on her, but deep into a gambling addiction, too. Not to mention everything going on with her graduation—damn, she had a lot on her plate, but she never let it show.

I knocked on my father's office door and stepped inside. On the table in front of him, a handful of pictures were scattered about. They were mostly of Tommy and me as kids.

"What are you doing?" I asked him, more than a little surprised. I had never really known him to be the sentimental type, but maybe his recent health problems had kick-started something in him I hadn't seen before.

"Just reminiscing," he told me. He didn't seem embarrassed about me seeing him like this. He really had changed. Normally, he would do anything he could to pretend he had never felt an emotion before in his life, but right now, he clearly wasn't bothered.

"About when we were young?" I asked, picking up one of the pictures. It was Tommy and me, hanging off the side of a swing together, both of us beaming big gummy smiles at the camera.

He nodded. "Yes, it's amazing how fast time has gone," he replied, shaking his head. "I feel like it was just yesterday you were this size and...well, look at you now."

"I bought you the money from Laurence," I told him, handing it over. I wanted to ride on this clear nostalgia he was having, hoping I could actually talk to him like a normal person for once. The two of us rarely took the time to just sit down together like this, and I knew I should have made more of an effort.

"Thank you," he replied. "You've been doing a good job lately, Joshua. Don't think I haven't noticed it. I know it feels like sometimes I go hard on you, but I know you're better than the shit you turn in sometimes, you know?"

I nodded. His words were harsh, but I could hardly argue with them. I had missed too many important deadlines to pretend I wasn't distracted, but I hoped I had proven myself in the time since his heart attack.

"Dad, can I ask you something?" I blurted out before I could stop myself. I didn't know if he was going to take this well, but I wanted to make sure I took the chance to say it out loud before I lost this moment.

"Yes, of course," he replied, looking surprised. "What is it?"

"Why are you always harder on me than Tommy?"

He paused for a moment, as though it wasn't something he had ever really considered before. I clenched my fist at my side. I wasn't angry, just tense. I knew a question like that might have been enough to set him off, and I didn't want to do something to impact his heart right now. Tommy would never have forgiven me.

Finally, he looked at me again.

"It's because I see so much of myself in you," he replied. "I see myself as a young man, and I think about how much better I could have done if there had just been someone there to kick my ass into gear."

"Dad, look around you," I told him. "You've already done better than most people do in their entire lives."

He smiled briefly. "Yes, but there was always more I could have done," he replied, a little wistful. I shook my head at him. Did he really think he was settling for less with the life he had now? I wished I could get him to see the enormity of his life and his legacy, but I supposed he was always going to be hard on himself. It was part of who he was, part of the reason he had managed to become the person he was today.

"I think you're doing pretty damn well," I replied. I didn't want him to think I saw him that way, as a man who could have done more if only he had tried. He was living a life most people could only dream of, and I wondered what it would take for him to feel he had done everything he was capable of.

"Thanks, son," he replied, and he leaned back in his chair for a moment and eyed me. "What about you? And the lawyer?"

"What about her?" I asked a little nervously. I didn't want him to tell me she wasn't welcome here anymore. I was already falling for her, and I knew if I had to keep her apart from my family, even for a little while, there was going to be serious trouble. I wanted to keep her close to me, and I didn't want to sacrifice the newfound respect I had gained from my father to do it.

"Are you going to marry her?"

The question caught me totally off guard, but I supposed I should have expected it. It wasn't often I brought women home, and now that I was getting a little older, it was natural he and Mom would be wondering if I was going to finally settle down and find someone to spend the rest of my life with. I didn't know what to say to that, but I paused and considered it for a moment.

Did I want to marry her? Hard to say. We didn't know each other well enough for me to say for certain that I wanted to make her my wife, but it wasn't exactly something I was willing to take off the table, either. We had an incredible connection, and even now, knowing some of what I did for a living, she hadn't run from me. There must have been something there, right? Something worth chasing after?

"I don't know," I replied finally. It was the best I could do for the time being. I wished I had a more concrete answer for him, but the truth was, I didn't have a clue. I cared for her, deeply, but she was so freshly out of a serious relationship, one where she was supposed to be getting married. Would she be so quick to turn around and marry me?

"You don't know?" my father asked, sounding incredulous. I shook my head.

"I have no idea," I admitted. "I like her, a lot. But I don't know if she's ready to get married yet."

"But you are, aren't you?" he asked.

I shrugged. I had been single a matter of months ago and thought I would be for a long time. Finding someone like her hadn't exactly been at the top of my list, but here I was, falling so hard for her it felt like everything else was just fading away from my mind.

"Well, you need to let me know when you make a decision," he told me, sighing as though he didn't want to keep having this conversation right now. I figured he had assumed I would have started talking marriage with her already. He and Mom were traditional that way, always wanting to make sure I was thinking of my future and what came next.

"I will," I promised him. I didn't know when that would be, but maybe I could broach the suggestion to her. I was sure it would come as something of a shock, but when she understood how important it was to my family, perhaps she would get that I wasn't just doing this to try and pressure her into something she wasn't ready for.

I wasn't her ex. I was never going to treat her the way Aaron did, even close to it. I owed her honesty. I needed to be upfront with what my family was going to expect from her if she stuck around for much longer, even if it was going to be tough to say all of that out loud.

I rose to my feet. I didn't want to spend too long with him; I had this incredible habit of finding a way to piss him off if we were together too long. I wasn't going to risk it, not with the state of his heart right now.

"I'm going to talk to Mom, okay?" I told him as I headed for the door.

"Yes, yes, she'll probably want to talk to you about the wedding too," he replied, waving his hand vaguely. I rolled my eyes, knowing he wasn't looking. They were already talking about it like she had a ring on her finger. We hadn't even spoken about the long-term yet, and I didn't know how she would react when I did.

I couldn't help but smile when I thought about her waiting for me back at my apartment. It wouldn't be long until I held her in my arms again, and I couldn't wait. Being around her did things to me nothing else did—it was like being on a high nobody could touch. I got drunk on her kisses, and I desperately needed a fix right now.

At least my family liked her. I figured my father wouldn't even be talking about all of this wedding stuff unless he thought there was something to her. It might have been way too soon for us to think about tying the knot, but when the time came—if it came—I wouldn't have to go through the pain of finding out if my family accepted her.

How could they not? She was amazing. I knew I wasn't going to find a better woman for me in this whole damn country.

And, all at once, the thought of marrying her suddenly made a lot more sense.

Chapter Eight

Amber

WHEN I WOKE THAT MORNING, I felt a flood of panic hit me. Oh, shit. Today was the day. And I didn't know how I was going to get through it.

My graduation day. I should have been excited, but there was a nagging worry at the back of my mind that warned me I had a lot to think about today, more than I wanted to. I looked around Josh's apartment, where the beautiful dress he had gotten for the day was hanging over the side of one of his chairs, and wondered how I was going to get through it without pissing someone off.

Because this was going to be the first time my parents had seen me since I had broken off the engagement with Aaron. They knew about it, of course, but it was one thing to be aware of what I had done and quite another to come to terms with it in any meaningful way. The way my mom had been talking, I was sure she thought I was about to go back to Aaron at any moment. She clearly had it in her head that this was nothing more than cold feet, and honestly, I wished I could get it through to her that I was serious. I didn't want anything to do with him again. I had someone new.

Someone who was coming with me to this graduation, actually. Josh was in the shower next door, and I could hear him humming happily to himself. He had told me how much he was looking forward to attending this ceremony with me, and there was no way I was going to go without him there by my side. No, I wanted him there, and I wanted to make sure I could look into the audience and see the man I cared for so deeply looking back at me.

Even if I had no idea how I was going to convince my parents he was actually good for me. They were going to take one look at him and make their minds up about the kind of person he was. I knew they wanted me with someone like Aaron, someone they could boast about to their friends and show off to the world. My mother had been so excited when he had proposed to me, probably more into it than I was, and I wished I could find some way to go back in time and tell her not to get too attached to the thought of him. He wouldn't be around for long. In fact, I wanted him gone from my head, from my family's memory as soon as possible, because I had a far better replacement on hand.

They weren't going to like Josh. I was sure of it. They had a certain image of the kind of man I should be with, and I wasn't stupid enough to think my new man met it. They would ask about his career, and he would have to slide away from their questions so as not to give away too much. I was sure he was already thinking of all the ways he could keep on their good side, but I wasn't sure it was going to be enough. I knew how judgmental my parents could be, and I didn't want him to feel bad for just sticking by me in the face of everything going on here.

I hadn't told him much about my family. Some sort of protective measure, I was pretty sure. I had already had a chunk of my life blown apart by finding out what Aaron had been up to, and I was more than a little worried I might discover more about my family than I wanted to know. If there was one thing being with Josh had taught me, it was that you never really knew what kind of secrets people had. Even the people closest to you.

Maybe it was why I felt so confident when I was with him. I didn't have to worry about anything because he had already shown me the secrets he would hide from the rest of the world. I knew what he did for a living, I knew what he was capable of, I knew what he had to do to stay in with his family. I had seen the way that Laurence guy had reacted to him, and I was sure it had come from some serious issues between them in the past.

Not to mention the man who had confronted us at the club. I hadn't gone delving for more from Josh on that, figuring it was behind us now, and he didn't even want to think about it, but I was curious to know what had gone down to cause such a crazy reaction. Josh couldn't hide that part of his life from me. I had seen too much. And people were not exactly bothered about keeping all of it to themselves, either. His past seemed to follow him around anywhere we went in this city.

I prayed it wasn't going to show its face at my graduation. I knew he would do what he could to keep his head down and not attract too much attention, making sure he didn't draw the focus away from me on my special day, but still—what if someone who hated him saw him there and decided to make a scene? I had no idea how I would navigate it. No idea how he would handle it. Though I had at least some idea of what my parents would do if they found out I was getting anywhere close to someone with his kind of history.

I needed to relax. This was supposed to be a good day for me, a triumphant day. I had worked my ass off to get here, and now, I was finally going to be done with my studies and able to get out into the real world. But it was hard for it to feel like a victory when so much seemed to be falling apart around me. My engagement, my best friend, my parents' confidence in me, given the way they had reacted to me ending things with Aaron. It felt as though I was struggling to keep it all together, hanging on by a thread trying to make sure I didn't lose control.

At least I had him. Josh emerged from the bathroom wearing a pair of slacks and an unbuttoned shirt, and I drank in the sight of him greedily. He was really gorgeous, no doubt about it, with those piercing blue eyes, that smile he gave me when he saw me looking.

"Like what you see?" he joked as he came over to plant a kiss on my cheek. "Good morning."

"Morning," I murmured back. I couldn't believe today was finally the day, but here it was. I needed to get myself together. At least I could make sure I looked good when I went out there. That had to count for something, didn't it?

"How you feeling?" he asked.

I shrugged. "I'm nervous," I admitted. "This isn't exactly how I pictured my graduation day going. I know my parents are going to have a whole lot to say..."

"Then they'll have to say it to me," he replied firmly, cupping my face in his hands. I smiled. I couldn't help it. When he was around, everything seemed to make a little more sense, even as I tried to piece together the bits of my life I couldn't make much sense of now.

"Thanks, Josh," I murmured, and I looked behind him to the dress he had purchased for me. The black one was for tonight, but the red number I had chosen for my graduation was just as lovely. I wanted to look my very best when I attended this ceremony, to make sure everyone knew I wasn't struggling or suffering just because my engagement was over. I mean, I was going to be turning up with a man a million times hotter than Aaron on my arm, anyway. If anyone thought Josh was a step down, they had another think coming.

"I guess I should start getting ready," I sighed as I pulled back the covers and planted my feet on the floor, but before I could go anywhere, Josh lifted his hand to get me to wait.

"Hold on a second," he told me. "There's something I want to give you."

"What?" I asked, confused. He had already given me so much, not least the dresses I was going to wear today. He didn't owe me anything else.

"I wanted to get you a little something to say congratulations for your graduation," he explained, as he reached over to the bedside table. I stared as he pulled out a large blue velvet box. What the heck had he done?

He popped it open, and I gasped when I saw what was waiting for me inside—the most beautiful diamond necklace, delicate and glittering in the soft morning light. I stared for a moment, not sure I was seeing this right.

"This...this is for me?" I asked, looking up at him again. I knew he was hardly going to snatch it out of my hands now that he had given it to me, but I couldn't quite believe I was deserving of something this beautiful, this exquisite.

"I thought it would go well with your bracelet," he told me, gently lifting it from the silk it was placed on and draping it around my neck. I allowed him to fasten it, feeling the slight weight of it against my skin. I looked down at the largest gem glimmering just between my collarbones and shook my head.

"This must have been crazy expensive," I told him.

"You're worth every cent," he replied, cupping my face in his hand. I couldn't believe he would really go out of his way to get me something like this, something so decadent and beautiful. I had never in a million years imagined anyone would want to gift me a piece of jewelry that likely could have paid my rent for several months.

"It's really beautiful," I told him, feeling a little flush come to my cheeks. I had never been with anyone who treated me the way he did. He seemed to view every little detail of me like it was the most precious thing in the world, waiting to be adorned with his gifts and presents and attention. I wasn't sure I would ever get used to someone treating me this way, but maybe I could at least give it a go now that the two of us were really doing this.

"Thank you," I murmured. It was the least I could say. I wished I had something to give him in return, but I figured I would be able to show him how much I loved my new gift once the two of us were alone together. It would give me something to look forward to once this long, long day was over, and I could hardly wait to just put it all behind me and move on to the next part.

As he rose to his feet to continue getting ready, I touched the necklace hanging around my neck. At least I would have something to show off to my parents, even if I wasn't sure they were going to love Josh. They would love what he could give to me, what he could do for me.

Maybe even half as much as I did.

Chapter Nine

Josh

I ADJUSTED MY TIE IN the mirror and looked myself up and down. Okay, yeah, I was pretty sure I could pass as a functioning member of society, at least for the day.

I could hear Amber listening to music as she got ready in the bathroom, and I grinned. I was so proud of her. I knew she had worked hard to get here, even harder when I considered what her fiancé had put her through, and she deserved to enjoy every single second of it.

I was going to meet her parents today, and I would have been lying if I said I wasn't a little nervous. I knew I should have known better than to let my nerves get the better of me, but I was sure they would have plenty to say about the kind of person I was, especially compared to Aaron. I didn't know how much they were aware of when it came to why Aaron and Amber had split, and I was sure there was some part of them wondering if they would get back together. If they were as waspy as Amber had made them out to be, they were likely going to expect her to drop me and marry him eventually. Couples like that, they don't like any kind of conflict, stuffing it all down until it's virtually unrecognizable and certainly hidden from the rest of the world. They would have likely encouraged Amber to stay with Aaron, even though it was obvious they were a terrible match.

We made a lot more sense, in some ways. The chemistry was there, the attraction—we could talk for hours and not run out of stuff to chat about, and I always found a smile on my face waking up beside her every morning. I needed her to know how serious I was about this. My father had put the idea of marriage in my head, and I wanted to discuss it with her before we got any further. I wanted to be sure she was on the same page, feeling the same connection I was. Impressing her parents would be a good way to secure it, to make sure she could see me as a more permanent part of her life.

In fact, I had planned a trip for the two of us as soon as her graduation was over. I hadn't told her about it, but I wanted it to come as a surprise, after how hard she had worked and everything she had done to get to where she was. She deserved a break, and I wanted to be the one to give it to her. I had booked us a luxury trip to Hawaii together, just a week or so, and I was certain she was going to love it. She'd mentioned off-hand that she hadn't had much time to travel since she and Aaron had been together, between her studies and his work, and I loved the idea of taking her somewhere fresh and exciting to let her blow off some steam. Plus, honestly, the vacation sex was going to be crazy. I could already feel it.

I checked my wallet to make sure the tickets were in there. I could have gotten the digital passes, but I liked the idea of being able to pull these out and hand them to her after we'd had dinner with her parents. I was still a little worried about meeting them, but I just had to promise myself I would make the most effort I could. I didn't have to be their best friend or anything; I just had to show them that I really cared about their daughter.

And hope they knew nothing of what my family did. Because I would have a way harder time convincing them I was worthwhile if they knew the truth about that.

I pulled on the Armani blazer I had picked out for the occasion and looked myself up and down in the mirror. Yeah, I looked pretty good. I wanted to blend into the crowd at this graduation, not draw anyone's attention. The chances of running into someone who had some beef with my family was slim, but never nil, so I wasn't intent on trying to pull focus today.

Besides, this was all about her. I wanted it to be a celebration of everything she'd achieved. I knew she was anxious about introducing me to her parents, but I would be the best boyfriend I possibly could be. I knew what they wanted to hear from me, and I just had to deliver on it long enough for them to ignore my dodging of the questions about my family. What they didn't know wouldn't hurt them, right?

I was about to put in my cufflinks when my phone rang. I answered it at once. As soon as I heard my father's voice down the line, my heart sank.

"Where are you?" he asked, sounding concerned. I didn't like him being so stressed out, not when I knew what had just happened to his heart. He needed to be as gentle on himself as possible, so I wouldn't snap back at him. I kept my voice as calm as I could.

"I'm at my place getting ready for Amber's graduation," I told him. "What's up?"

"I need you to head down to the pier to meet with Goncharov," he told me quickly. "He's bringing in some goods tonight, and we need to make sure we pick them up and get them stashed before the cops get there."

My heart dropped. There was no way I was going to flake out on Amber's big day. Tommy had to be around, didn't he? And he wouldn't want me to miss out on this...

"Isn't there someone else who can handle this?" I asked him. "I promised Amber I would be there. I don't want to let her down."

"I wouldn't be asking you if there was someone else," he replied, sounding annoyed. I tried not to bristle in annoyance at the way he was speaking to me. I knew he wasn't trying to be an asshole, but honestly, the way he was talking right now, it was hard not to get a little pissed. He was making it clear he would have much rather had someone else take care of this instead of me. I was the last resort for him.

I rubbed my hand over my face. I should have a better answer for him, but I knew I couldn't blow him off. I had just been getting back into his good books, and if I blew him off now, he was going to turn it all around and go back to being just as mad at me as he had been before. I couldn't lose the goodwill I had built up, but I didn't want to let down Amber, either. My head was spinning as I tried to make sense of what I wanted to do next.

"How long is it going to take?" I asked.

"Should be finished by midday," he replied. I looked at my watch. I might miss some of the ceremony, but I would be back in time to meet her parents and play the dutiful boyfriend. If I could manage it while also keeping my father happy, I would consider it a downright miracle.

"Joshua, are you going to do this for me or not?" The tension was obvious in his voice. I hated this. I didn't want to have to mess up the day I had planned for her, but I didn't see how I could get out of this without letting my father down.

"I'll do it," I replied, finally, dredging up some motivation from deep down inside of me and hoping for the best. I just wanted to be back with Amber already, and the sooner I took care of whatever it was my father wanted, I would be able to. I hadn't told him about the trip I had planned with her, but hopefully, if I got some goodwill on my side from this, I wouldn't have to worry about spending a few days away.

"Good," he replied. "I'll send you the address."

He didn't bother to thank me. This was, to him, the bare minimum I could do to prove myself after how much I had let him down lately. I had hoped our conversation the other night might have been enough to convince him the two of us had more in common than we lacked, but I clearly hadn't quite gotten there yet.

He hung up the phone, and a moment later, my phone buzzed once more with the arrival of the address he was going to send me to. I could still hear Amber in the bathroom, and I frowned at the thought of having to tell her I wasn't going to be able to make it to her graduation.

No, that wasn't true. I would. I was just going to be running a little late. I was going to be there for her, I wasn't going to let her down, not on a day I knew meant so much to her. I wasn't going to flake on meeting her parents when I knew how much she wanted me to be there. She deserved a boyfriend who would support her at every turn, and I wasn't going to fail on that when I had spent so much time trying to convince her I was different than her ex.

When she emerged from the bathroom, I almost groaned. She looked so damn good, and I had to leave and go somewhere else right now instead of stripping her down and fucking her right then and there on the spot.

"What do you think?" she asked, and I smiled as I looked her up and down.

"You look gorgeous," I assured her. "I'm going to be coming to the ceremony a little after you, okay? I have something to take care of for my dad."

"Oh," she replied, her brow furrowing. "I—will you be there, though?"

"Of course I will," I promised her. "I'm not going to miss this. I just need a little time to handle this, and I'll be with you."

She nodded. She still looked a little doubtful. After being let down so many times by her ex, it didn't surprise me she was having a hard time believing me. I kissed her on the lips, clasping her face in my hands.

"I promise," I told her again. "Really. I mean it. I'm going to be there."

"I know," she replied, and she sounded like she believed me. I had a car coming to pick us up, and I intended it for her so she could have a luxury ride to her ceremony.

"The car'll be here in about ten minutes," I explained to her. "You take it. I'll find my own way there."

She nodded. She still looked a little freaked. I didn't blame her. We'd had a plan in place, and now I was in the process of screwing it up. I didn't want her to think I was trying to get out of this. I needed her to know I was as committed to being with her as anything else in my life, and that meant getting whatever my father needed over and done with as soon as I could.

I almost told her about the tickets in my wallet, but I thought better of it. I wanted it to be a surprise for her, something we could share when all of this was over and done with. It might not have been easy to keep it from her when I knew it would have made me walking out that much easier, but I could hold back, at least for now. I could give her some time to focus on her graduation.

"You'll be back before dinner, right?" she asked me.

"Of course I will," I replied, and I clasped her face in my hands and kissed her. I wished I didn't have to let her go, but with everything happening right now, I didn't have much of a choice.

"I'll be back as soon as I can," I promised her. "Now you go and enjoy your day, all right?"

"You're going to be okay, aren't you?" she asked, doubt and concern visible on her face. I nodded.

"I'm going to be just fine," I assured her, trying my best to soothe her into believing me. I knew it wasn't easy for her to take what I was saying at face value, but I needed her to try.

"Okay," she murmured. I could tell she didn't believe me, but this was the best I could do for her right now. I didn't want her diving too deep into her own doubts and worries. This was about her, her day to shine and show off everything she had achieved, and there was no way I was going to let any of my shit get in the way of it.

"I'll see you soon," I replied, and I kissed her cheek again and turned for the door. Hopefully, I could get this over with in a matter of hours and make it back to the ceremony.

And if not? If not, I was going to have to make a choice between her and my father. And I wasn't sure my family was going to be too happy with who came out on top.

Chapter Ten

Amber

I CAST MY GAZE AROUND the room again, chewing my lip as I looked for him. Where the hell was he? How long was it going to take for him to get here?

It was just past midday, and Josh still hadn't turned up to the ceremony. He hadn't missed anything particularly interesting. In fact, it had mostly been droning guest speakers the entire time, as well as a few awards given out to the suck-ups who had spent their time trying to get on the professors' good side. They hadn't even started giving out diplomas yet, but I still wanted him here when it happened.

My parents were in their assigned seats, Dad looking like he was about to drop off on the spot while Mom fanned herself with a program. I knew they probably wanted this to be over as much as I did. They had already found out they were going to be meeting my new boyfriend today, and I could tell they were in a rush to make sure they got to that point already.

Mom was still mad as all hell I had broken up with Aaron. I hadn't given her the gory details, and she was still hanging on to the belief I was going to get back together with him. I wished I could just tell her everything, but I wasn't sure she would have even believed me if I'd told her. She had always held Aaron in such high esteem, I think it would have been tough for her to acknowledge he might not have been the guy she thought he was.

I had no idea what she was going to make of Josh. She didn't know anything about him so far, and I wanted to keep it that way. I was sure she would have had a million comments for him if she got the chance, making sure I knew just what she thought of him. I didn't want to let it get to me, but it was going to be hard, when I knew she would do everything she could to negatively compare him to Aaron.

I didn't even want to think of them in the same sentence. I knew there might have been a little overlap, but it didn't mean there was any reason to compare them. Josh was a million times the man Aaron had been, in the way he treated me and everything else, too. His kindness, his thoughtfulness, his sweetness when it came to me seemed to make everything a little easier. I loved being around him, loved seeing the soft look on his face when he gazed at me, as though he could hardly believe someone like me had decided to spend time with a man like him. I wished I could show him a little more clearly how hard I was falling for him, but I figured the most important thing now was sticking around and showing him that his job wasn't going to be a problem for me.

Well, it wasn't going to be a problem as long as he turned up here today. It wasn't even that I minded him having to take care of whatever family emergency his father had asked him to deal with, but it was knowing something might have gone wrong and led to him getting hurt that freaked me out the most. I hated thinking about him out there facing down something he might not be able to handle.

I couldn't stop wondering if something had happened to him. I knew I wouldn't be able to handle it. Even the thought of him hurt was enough to send a shockwave of fear and anger through my body. I had to soothe myself, remind myself he had been doing this for way, way longer than he had known me, and he wasn't going to get himself into anything he couldn't manage. It was one of the things I respected so much about him, his ability to take anything that came his way.

I still wished he was here. If he was here, in the assigned seat I had gotten for him, then I would know for certain there was nothing for me to worry about, and I could actually relax for a change. As it was, it felt as though my heart was going to drop right out of my stomach, vanish into my polished high heels. I had wanted him here, and knowing he wasn't around was starting to get to me more than I wanted to admit to.

The names started being called, and I did my best to clap and look impressed at everyone who went up. I knew I might be working with some of these people in the near future, given that we were all going into a similar field, and the last thing I needed was to piss some of them off and make a fool of myself. As far as they were concerned, I was happier for their own graduation than for my own, and I wanted to keep it that way.

By the time I was headed up to the stage to pick up my diploma, my stomach was churning. I wasn't just worried about falling over or something, like I might have been before I met Josh, but I was scared for where he was, what he was doing right now. His absence was strong in my head as I looked out over the audience, scanning it to see if he was there.

No sign of him. I smiled and shook hands with the head of my department and turned to go back down the steps, hoping against hope he would be there soon. I wasn't sure how much longer I could go, and I ached at the thought of being without him any longer. It just didn't seem fair. I wanted to be with him right now, I wanted him here so he could celebrate this moment with me, but he wasn't, and I didn't know what kind of chance I stood of him turning up at the last moment to show me he wanted to be here at all.

I took a deep breath as I sat down. It wasn't about him wanting to be here—he'd wanted it. It was just that something had happened to get in the way of it. I wasn't going to blame him when I knew he couldn't help not being here with me right now. He had gotten me this gorgeous necklace, and I touched the cool metal around my throat, trying my best to remind myself why I still trusted in him so much. He had made so much of an effort, and I would be the worst kind of asshole to brush it off and act like I didn't notice it.

By the time the ceremony was over, I was so glad to be able to go be with my parents. I wanted them here with me right now, wanted nothing more than to celebrate the occasion. I knew I should have been more focused on myself and what I was achieving here, but it was hard to keep that in mind when all I wanted was for the man I loved to be here with me.

"Oh, honey, you've done so well," Mom remarked as she adjusted a strand of hair next to my ear. She never seemed satisfied with how I looked, always finding some way to switch it up or work on me to meet her standards. Sometimes, I thought about calling her out on it, but right now, I was too exhausted to think of anything like that.

"Thank you," I replied as Dad pulled me into a hug. I was glad they were here, I was, but there was someone missing. I pulled back and looked around the room once more, praying Josh would have turned up, but there was no sign of him at all. I chewed my lip. I didn't like the way this was going. He had told me he was going to be here, and I had wanted to trust him beyond anything else. If something bad had happened, I didn't know how I was going to take it...

"You okay?" Mom asked, and I nodded quickly.

"Yeah, yeah, I'm fine," I replied, plastering as big a smile on my face as I could muster. "Just...a little overwhelmed, that's all. I can't believe I'm really doing this, after all this time."

"Well, you deserve it," Dad replied, squeezing my shoulder as he smiled at me. I felt tears prick my eyes and did my best to push them down. I didn't want this day to be overtaken by the emotion I was feeling because Josh wasn't here. It would have been so rude to brush off my parents being with me right now, especially because they had supported me every step of the way to make it here.

"What about this new man of yours?" Mom asked, her eyes darting this way and that as though she thought he might be hiding behind a potted plant or something.

"He's...he had a family emergency," I told her. It was close enough to the truth, wasn't it? Close enough to count. I didn't want this to turn into some deconstruction of our relationship, when it had only just started.

"Oh, I see," my father replied. I could hear a little iciness in his voice. This wasn't how I wanted him to get to know Josh, but it wasn't as though I could just magic him up out of the blue and make it so he had been here all along. I was worried about his absence, sure, but I was more worried about how my parents were going to react to it. They might think of him as some sort of flake, and I knew he was anything but. He really cared about me, really gave a shit about how my life was going, and if he wasn't here, then he must have had a damn good reason for it.

I just needed to get to the bottom of it.

"Well, we have a table booked for dinner," Mom remarked. "Even if he's not coming with us, we should get going. I don't want to be late."

"Right," I agreed, and I rubbed my hand over my face. Damn, I was so tired all of a sudden. I knew I should be able to hold it together a little better, especially on a day like this, but without Josh by my side to help me, it all felt impossible. He was the one I relied on in situations like this, the one I wanted to be here more than anyone else. He knew what I had been through to end up at this point, and my parents didn't know a thing about Aaron cheating on me with Kimmy or his gambling addiction. I wasn't sure I wanted to bring down the night by talking about it, but if they were going to keep asking questions about Josh, I might not have a choice but to come up with some sort of answer.

"Do you want to get changed?" Mom asked, her gaze sweeping up and down my dress. The other outfit I'd had picked out for today was back at the apartment, and I didn't feel like going all the way back there to change into something Josh likely wasn't even going to see me in. I could still remember the way his face had lit up when he had caught sight of me in that dress, and I felt a twist of annoyance knowing I wasn't going to be able to show off to him in it.

There would be other times. I had to remind myself of that. He was in this for the long haul, and he had done all he could to prove it to me. I wasn't going to forget everything he had done for me so far, all the ways he had come through for me when nobody else would have. He cared about me, really cared about me, and he wanted me to be happy. Whatever was keeping him from me right now, I was sure it was important, or he wouldn't have been there taking care of it.

I plastered a big smile on my face, hoping I could cloak the doubt in my system right now with some brightness. I didn't want to remember this day as the one Josh had missed. There was so much for me to celebrate, so much for me to be proud of, and I didn't want to lose out on enjoying it.

"No, I'm good," I told her. "Let's get out of here. I'm starving."

Chapter Eleven

Josh

I CLENCHED MY FISTS on the table in front of me. I wasn't sure what it was going to take to get this guy to see things from my perspective, but he was starting to piss me off in a big way, and I didn't know how long I could contain myself while he sat there smugly opposite me.

Ansel Gregori was the man on the other side of the table, an arms smuggler we'd been working with for years. But I could see why my father had decided I needed to come down here and do something about him right now. He was acting up, and we couldn't let anyone get in the way of our business. We had to keep our grip on the city, and he was deliberately trying to make it hard for us.

I had a feeling it had to do with my father's heart attack. The way Ansel had been talking since I had arrived, making reference to the struggles my family had been dealing with lately, it was obvious he wanted to hit us while we were down. But he had a whole other think coming if he thought he could palm me off this easily.

He was offering to sell us the guns at a ridiculously inflated rate, so big it would have been nigh-on impossible to make any kind of money off of them. I knew I should have known better than to let him get under my skin, but I was getting seriously pissed. Every second that ticked by was another I would be late for Amber's graduation, and I didn't want to let her down. I was supposed to be meeting her parents today, for shit's sake, and if I flaked out on that, it would be hard to get back in their good books.

"I've made my deal clear to you," Ansel told me as he spread his hands wide on the table again. "You need to make a choice. You either accept what I'm offering or I find someone else who's going to take care of it."

"You're just doing this because you think my father's weak," I spat back at him, utterly derisive. "You're using him. You wouldn't dare pull something like this if you thought he had the strength to stand up to you."

"But it looks like he doesn't," Ansel replied, his voice cool. I bristled. He had no idea what my father was capable of. My dad was a million times the man and the businessman he would ever be, and for him to come in here and act like a pig was starting to get to me.

I leaned across the table, narrowing my eyes at him, making it as clear as I could that I wasn't going to put up with this. "You sell to us on our usual plan," I told him. "Or..."

"Or what?" he asked, grinning widely. He knew he had us backed into a corner. We couldn't risk not being able to meet the supply his guns would have given to us, but I didn't want to give him the satisfaction of knowing it for sure. He needed to pull himself together, act like an honest man again. Or at least, as honest as someone in his line of work could be.

I looked down at my watch and bit back a groan of irritation. I had officially missed her graduation now. I might still be able to make the dinner they were having afterwards, but I hadn't been there in the crowd to see her graduate, and I knew it wasn't something she was going to forget about anytime soon. Why should she? She had expected me to be there, I had promised her over and over again I wouldn't let her down, but now I had. I hated this. I felt another surge of anger launch through me upon figuring out what a mess he had made of my day, and I was about to lunge for him when someone strolled into the room.

"Ansel," Tommy greeted our dealer as he took the seat next to me. I didn't know when he had decided to show up, but it was probably for the best. He'd likely had to deal with a whole lot more of this shit than I had over the past few years, and I had no doubt he would do better at keeping his head than me. I didn't like having to hand it over to someone else like this, but I didn't see what other choice I had. When it came to people like Gregori, I would lash out before I could stop myself, and a mistake like that could cost me everything.

"What are you doing here?" I muttered. I wasn't sure I wanted him just turning up like this, as though it was the most natural thing in the world. I had thought I had this all under control, but more than ever, it seemed like it was impossible for me to handle.

"I heard you were down here, thought you could use some help," he muttered to me under his breath. Couldn't he have done this sooner, so I could have made Amber's graduation? I knew he wouldn't want to hear about anything to do with my girlfriend, but still. It felt like the least I deserved for dropping everything to handle this for Dad.

"What's the problem here?" he asked Ansel, and he spilled the details at once. I couldn't believe he had the nerve to just tell him like that, as though he was in the right. Tommy nodded as he listened, not interrupting him or trying to argue. I didn't know how he could stay so cool right now. I wanted to go for the guy.

Once he was done, Tommy leaned forward calmly, his hands clasped on the table in front of him. I expected him to start chewing him out, but instead, he just offered him a decent alternative.

"Look, I get it, man," he assured him. "I know how hard it is out there right now. But these prices you're asking for—you're not going to be able to sell them to anyone else. How about we add ten percent to our usual price?"

Ansel's eyes darted between the two of us, as though he was doubtful of what Tommy was saying. After how intense I had been with him,

I wasn't surprised to see he was kind of doubtful about going along with something like this.

But he probably realized Tommy had a point with what he was telling him. He could go ahead and demand as much as he wanted, but at the end of the day, he needed to shift his product, and we were the best chance he had of doing it. He nodded slowly, extending his hand to Tommy.

"I'll take it," he replied, and Tommy took his hand and shook firmly. I let out a sigh of relief. Thank goodness. I didn't want to have to be here for another second, not when I knew that Amber was out there and likely waiting for me to turn up like I had promised I would.

We went our separate ways when the deal was done, and I checked my watch again. Amber would already be at dinner with her parents, and I wasn't sure I wanted to risk crashing it after I had already managed to screw up today so royally.

"You okay?" Tommy asked, noticing my discomfort.

"I'm...I'm fine," I replied, shaking my head. "It was Amber's graduation today. Ansel made me miss the whole thing."

I didn't want to add, of course, that if Tommy had bothered to show up a little sooner, I might have made it. I was sure he didn't want to hear it. I knew he had been busy too since Dad had gotten sick, and he wasn't flaking out just for the sake of it. If he couldn't make it, it was because he had genuinely had shit he needed to take care of, and he didn't need me snapping at him over something he couldn't help.

"I'm sure she'll understand," he remarked. He didn't sound particularly bothered by it. He had never dated much, and I was sure he didn't really understand how serious this was. I had let her down, and if there was one thing I didn't want to do, it was let her down. I needed to prove how much better I was than her ex, a man who had fucked her around every chance he had gotten. I prayed she would understand why I had done what I had done.

I didn't want this to come between us, but with things so early on in our relationship, I wasn't certain I was going to be able to keep her from seeing it that way. I needed her to believe I hadn't skipped out on her graduation just to hurt her. I would never have done something like that, not in a million years. I checked my phone to see if she had been in touch, but there was nothing. I sighed.

"Come on, let's get a drink," Tommy told me, throwing an arm around my shoulders as though he could sense how unhappy I was in that instant.

"Sure," I replied. I knew there was no point trying to go to meet with her parents for dinner, I had already screwed it up beyond belief. They probably didn't want to hear a thing I had to say anymore, and it stung to think of how much I was letting her down.

He took me to a bar I'd never been to before, a dive place with sticky floors and cheap beers. I was surprised he even knew about a place like this. He always seemed to have a taste for the finer things when we were out together, but I guessed sometimes he had to accept a lesser version when he was heading to parts of the city like this one. Maybe it was an opportunity, too, to brush aside some of his usual status, to make sure the people here were seeing him as nothing more than another paying customer as opposed to someone they needed to bend over backwards to please. Yeah, sometimes it's nice to get the special treatment, but sometimes, you just want to be handled like anyone else.

He ordered us a couple of beers, and I retreated back to a table far from the door, wanting to hide out in this place as best I could. I felt like such a failure for the way I had let Amber down today, and I just hoped she would be able to forgive me and accept that I hadn't done this to hurt her. It was truly out of my hands.

"How do you deal with it?" I asked Tommy once we were a couple of beers in and I was feeling a little looser in the tongue. He raised his eyebrows at me.

"Deal with what?"

"Balancing the family stuff with everything else going on in your life," I replied, waving vaguely. "I—I feel like I've just been trying to juggle it all and not getting anywhere with it. I can't find time for both of them."

He snorted, as though surprised I was even asking that question.

"You really think I have a life outside what Dad wants from me?" he pointed out. I hadn't even considered that, but I supposed he had a point. After all, he had committed his entire adulthood to making sure he was on my father's good side, and I supposed there was something to be said for it. Our father had always compared me to him, but maybe it was as simple as making the family my priority. My only priority.

"I've never really dated anyone, not seriously," he continued, sipping on his beer as he spoke. He didn't seem bothered by admitting this to me, as though he knew he had nothing to be ashamed of. I had never even heard him mention dating a girl before, even as I cast my mind all the way back to high school. Had it really been that long for him? I supposed it would explain how he always seemed to be able to handle whatever mess our family was in because he didn't have anything on the outside to draw his attention away.

"Don't you miss it?" I wondered aloud. "Or feel like you're missing out on something?"

He shrugged again.

"I don't feel like I'm missing out on anything," he replied. "Nothing to miss out on when I don't even know what's out there. Besides, the chances of finding someone I like who's cool with this work is pretty slim."

The words hung in the air between us, as though he was daring me to argue with him. Did he want to know if Amber had accepted my work yet? I hadn't asked her outright, but she had been around my family enough that she surely understood it on some level. She wasn't fighting me too hard on it, so I figured she didn't mind it. It might be different when her parents found out what I did, but I would deal with that when it happened. For now, all that mattered was making sure she was comfortable enough to stick around.

"Yeah, it is," I agreed. The fact that Amber hadn't turned her back on me and declared she never wanted to see me again after what she had seen with Aaron was downright close to a miracle, and I refused to allow anything to dissuade me of it. She had seen some of the darker side of it, and she hadn't gone anywhere. She still wanted to be by my side.

For now, at least.

I lifted the beer to my lips as I pondered it. How long would she stick around? And how long could I balance the two sides of my life before one got the better of the other? I had no idea, and I didn't like the thought of finding out.

But today had been a reminder of how hard it was to balance my family and Amber. I had commitments to them both, but letting one down would mean accepting a dent to my image, even if I was just doing it to help out with the other. There was too much going on in my life right now for me to make sense of, and the longer it took me to figure out the balance, the more trouble I was going to have in the meantime.

And damn, I'd had enough trouble today.

Chapter Twelve

Amber

I SMOOTHED DOWN THE skirt of the black dress and looked out over the city below me. Just where the hell was Josh right now? And what were the chances he was going to be sober when he walked back through that door?

I sighed to myself. I had just made it back from dinner and changed into the black dress Josh had practically begged me to wear. I thought I would feel beautiful in it, but instead, it looked ridiculous. All dressed up with nowhere to go. I was totally humiliated, and I hated how much I had let it get to me.

My parents had been dropping hints about the nonexistent man who was supposed to be by my side all night long, and I honestly wasn't sure how much more of it I could take. In truth, I had prayed he was going to turn up just to prove them wrong, but he hadn't. No; instead, he had just left me without so much as a call or a text to let me know where he was, letting me worry my heart out as I tried to work out what had happened to him.

I wanted to scream. By now, I was seriously pissed. If something had happened to him, I was sure I would have heard about it by now, which meant he had just decided to swoop off and do whatever he wanted on the day he was supposed to be at my graduation. My diploma was on the table next to me, perched on top of his balcony, but I wanted to toss it down into the street below for all it meant. Josh should have been there, and he wasn't. How was that supposed to make me feel?

I reached for the glass of wine I had poured myself from his liquor cabinet. I was sure drinking wasn't a good idea, given I'd already had a couple with dinner, but I wanted something to take the edge off the anger and grief I was feeling at that moment. Maybe grief was too strong a word for it, but it seemed close—the deep sadness I felt knowing Josh had decided to flake out on what he had promised me. He had told me he would be back soon, and instead, he had left me looking like a damn idiot.

I wasn't going to forget this soon. He'd better have a damn good reason as to why he hadn't turned up. He had told me it was serious, or at least the way he acted had communicated it, but what could go on so long it would keep him from even dropping by for dessert? He had chosen to skip out on every part of this, and I would have been lying if I said I wasn't beyond pissed to know he had made the choice to leave me to get through it alone.

My parents would never look at him the same way, not now. No, from this point on, he would always be the guy who had skipped out on my graduation, even though he'd promised he was going to be there. My dad had peppered the conversation with questions about him, but my mom had clearly not wanted to hear about him at all. I could tell she was passing judgment in her mind, ready to hit me with all of it if I gave her the chance.

I had wanted today to be perfect. I knew he had other responsibilities, but did he have to stand me up like that, make me look like such an idiot? I was sure I deserved a little more than to be brushed off like a pain in his ass he didn't want to have to deal with.

This dress had been meant for him. I knew I would never be able to wear it now without thinking about what he had done to me, and it fucked me up to think about how much fun we could have had if he had just bothered to show his face when he said he would.

I tugged it down a little farther and looked toward the door again. It was nearly ten now, and he still wasn't back. Where the hell was he?

I couldn't help but wonder if he had bumped into another girl when he had been out, if he had found someone he liked more than me. I tried not to linger on it, but the notion was getting hard for me to brush off. The two of us had hooked up in a club a matter of days ago. What if someone else made a move on him and he didn't turn them down...?

All at once, the door opened, and I felt a mixture of anger and relief when I saw Josh walking in. He was stumbling slightly, obviously drunk, and it took him a second to work out where the hell I was. When he looked up and saw me sitting there, waiting for him, he strode toward me with all the confidence of a man who was too drunk to realize he had made a bigger mistake than he could charm himself out of.

"There you are," he greeted me, and he leaned down to kiss me on the lips. I turned my head so he had no choice but to press it against my cheek instead. I was pissed at him and didn't want him to think I was suddenly playing along with what he had done to me.

"How was your graduation?" he asked as he slumped down into the seat opposite me. I could smell cheap beer clinging to him, and I glared straight ahead.

"It was fine," I muttered. "Except you weren't there."

"Yeah, sorry about that," he replied dismissively, as though he couldn't have cared less. Was he really going to treat it as though it didn't matter? I wanted to turn around and grab him by the shoulders and ask him if he was really doing this, but I figured it would have been stupid to ask for more than he was giving me. I wanted to see his true reaction, find out how much he really cared and how much had just been a front he put on.

"What were you doing all day?" I asked, shooting a look over to him as I held my glass of wine even closer. I wanted his reasoning. If there was something good enough to satisfy me, maybe I would be able to forgive him. Some part of me wanted that, wanted to be able to let this go so we could just return to how we'd been before, but I doubted it would be so easy.

"I was dealing with something for my father," he replied.

"All day?" I shot back. "And at a bar? I can smell the beer on you."

He turned to me slowly. I could tell this line of questioning was annoying him, but he should have come up with something better if he wanted me to drop it. I wasn't going to let him palm me off with some bullshit just because he didn't see this as something I had a right to be mad about.

"Tommy and I went out for some drinks afterwards," he replied. Afterwards? When had this been? When he could have been meeting my parents? What had he been thinking? I tried to control my breathing, not wanting to come off as crazy but finding it hard to chill in the face of what he was telling me.

"You were supposed to be at my graduation today," I reminded him. "And meeting my parents. You stood me up."

"Amber, I had something I needed to take care of," he shot back at me, his voice edged with annoyance. "I told you when I left I wouldn't be doing this unless it was really important. Okay?"

I bit back a snort of derision. Drinking beers with Tommy had been that important he couldn't keep his commitments to me? Did he really think I was going to take that shit? I had been there for him with his family stuff, and now, he had all but left me out in the cold and let me deal with his mess alone. How was it fair? How was it right?

"I just wanted you to be there," I told him, my voice a little sharper than I had intended it to be. I could tell he was annoyed, not even looking at me as he replied.

"And I just want you to understand that sometimes, there's things that are bigger than you and me," he replied. I looked over at him, my eyes wide. This was the first I was hearing of it.

"You mean that?" I asked.

"I have a lot to deal with when it comes to my family, you know that," he replied, shaking his head. He was still staring at the city below us, like he couldn't even bring himself to make eye contact with me.

"And you need to understand, whatever's going on in your life, there are times I'm going to have to make them my priority," he continued. He was speaking as though this was stuff I should already have known, and I would have been lying if I said I wasn't pissed as hell hearing it. After all I had done for him, all I had given up for him, he was basically telling me I should be grateful for what little I was getting from him? Yeah, it didn't feel right. Not one little bit. And he had another think coming if he thought I was just going to stand back and let him do that to me.

"I'm not asking you to forget about them altogether," I argued back. "I just...I wanted you there today, and you didn't even make the effort."

"So you don't understand, then," he replied belligerently, looking back at me. "You don't understand how important this is."

"Josh, I've tried to be here for you with your family since the start," I reminded him. "I know how hard it's been for you. I just...I really, really wanted you there. And you weren't."

"Because I didn't want to bust in late and make a bad impression," he shot back.

"So you thought it would be better not to turn up at all?" I demanded, gesturing with my glass of wine. I couldn't believe he was doing this to me, making me feel like the crazy one who was acting entitled. He had promised me today, and now he was hardly even offering an apology for not turning up.

He didn't reply. Fine—if he was going to be like that about it, I didn't have to sit around here and take it. I knew better than to put all my hopes in him given the way he had let me down today. If he wanted to act like an ass, then he could act like an ass. I wasn't going to listen to any more. I had already dealt with a guy who'd continually brushed me off, and I didn't want this thing with Josh to turn into a repeat of that.

I was going to go back to my place and take some time to think. I had jumped into things pretty fast with Josh, and maybe this was a reminder to pull it back just a little, focus on my own life again. After all, I had just graduated; this was supposed to be about me.

I was gathering my stuff, calling a cab, and finishing up the wine when I spotted the tickets on the table. One of them had my name on it, which caught my attention, and when I went in for a closer look and saw what they actually were, my jaw dropped.

They were tickets to Hawaii. For Josh and me. Leaving tomorrow. I peered down at them, sure I was seeing this wrong, but there was no mistaking what they were. My heart twisted. Had he gotten those for us? So we could take some time away and just hang out together? Maybe he had wanted to surprise me with them tonight, but as soon as he had come through the door, I had just started ragging on him.

I looked back out to the balcony, where he was still sitting, staring down across the city. It was obvious he didn't want to talk to me right now, and I wasn't going to push for anything more than I had already gotten from him. I needed to give him some space, even if I wanted more than anything to just stay with him right now, take these tickets in and ask him if he'd really meant it when he had gotten these.

But it didn't undo what had happened. Maybe it was for the best if we took a little time to ourselves to work this out. I didn't want to rush this and wind up ruining something amazing just because I was hurrying to get somewhere we didn't even need to be.

I heard the cab arrive downstairs and hurried out of the apartment before I could say or do anything else. I didn't want to turn this into a bigger fight than it had to be, though it already seemed more serious than I could make sense of. I didn't understand why he couldn't just tell me what I wanted to hear, that he was sorry and he would try harder in the future. Why did he have to come in posturing about how much more important his family was to him than me...?

As I climbed into the back of the cab, I shoved those thoughts down. Better not to let them take root in my mind right now. I wanted to talk to him, but I needed to calm down a little first, and I was sure he did, too.

This was the first major disagreement the two of us had had since we had gotten together, and honestly, it had shaken me. Things had been going so well, and now this had dropped in out of nowhere like an anvil on our heads.

As soon as I was back at my place, I called his number. I just wanted to let him know I had gotten there safely and he had nothing to worry about. But I didn't get a response, and the silence thrummed in my head as I put my phone down.

How long was he going to make me wait before he got back to me? He knew I must have been worried, but he didn't seem to care. Whatever he was doing right now, he didn't want me to be a part of it.

And maybe I should take the hint and give him his space. We could talk about this in the morning.

Even if falling asleep without him was more painful than I could fathom right now.

Chapter Thirteen

Josh

I STARED DOWN OVER the city and did my best to contain the anger that was threatening to get the better of me.

I was pissed at myself for letting her get so far under my skin, but there was nothing I could do to shake her loose. Much as I wanted to be able to put it all aside, I knew there was no way in hell I could just fix the fight we'd had. She'd left, for goodness sake, before I'd even had a chance to give her the tickets.

She would have turned me down, I was sure of it. She was too angry about everything that had happened today to see that I meant well. Maybe I shouldn't have been so defensive, but when she came for my family like that, what other choice did I have? I wasn't going to let her talk shit about them. I wasn't going to let her make me feel bad for going to help them out when they needed me.

I knew I had done the right thing, whether or not she would ever be able to admit it. Yeah, I knew I had let her down, but surely she could see why it was more important for me to take care of family stuff. There could have been a damn turf war across all of Chicago if I hadn't stepped in to do something about it, and missing her graduation was the price I had to pay.

I could have handled it if she had been a little less mad at me. But I had walked in here and had to deal with her turning on me like I had done all this on purpose, when what I needed was a little understanding from the woman who was supposed to be my partner. Maybe it was too soon to expect this level of understanding from her, but couldn't she see how crazy she was acting? I hadn't wanted to turn up late to meet her parents. It would have been better just to re-schedule and find a day where I wasn't in the middle of some serious drama around my father and his business. I didn't want to be stressed out of my mind. I wanted to make a good impression on them.

She had tried calling me, but I hadn't picked up the phone. I didn't want to speak to her yet. In fact, I didn't want to be sitting around this apartment, pretending I was okay when all I wanted was to forget about what had just happened and move on to something else.

I wanted to get out of here. I couldn't stay here without thinking of her. I knew I should have done more to keep her there, but I didn't know what I could do. She obviously thought I had fucked up, and maybe she was right.

I needed to get another drink. I had been out at that shitty bar with Tommy all evening, but I wanted somewhere new, somewhere I wasn't going to run into my brother. I knew he would have turned me right around and told me to go back to her, and I didn't want to deal with his judgment in the face of everything else right now.

Maybe he had a point. Maybe I should have kept my head down and stayed out of trouble when it came to women. There was no way for me to fuck up a relationship if I didn't have one, right? He might have been lonely, but he was focused. He knew what he needed to hold in the front of his mind at all times, and he didn't let his focus waver.

As I headed down to the nearest bar I could find, I wondered if I should do the same thing. Forget about Amber. Maybe there was no way I could balance the two sides of my life. I was always going to have to sacrifice one or the other, and my family was what I needed to keep in focus here. Yes, I cared for her, I really did, but I knew my father's empire was guaranteed to set me up for the rest of my life.

I thought it would have been enough to set Amber up, too, but it didn't seem to be enough for her. Did she realize how serious this was? If I hadn't been there to keep things from boiling over, the whole city could have dropped into chaos. I was sure if she had given me a chance to explain—

Nah, I wouldn't have given her the details. I was sure she would have freaked if she discovered I was involved with arms dealers. She had been able to keep out of the heavier stuff, but something like this, it would have made it impossible for her to deny the truth. Much as she might have wanted to, she wouldn't have been able to ignore how dark things got around here.

I didn't want to drag her into this. But I still wanted her in my life. I didn't know how I could balance the two sides of that, but I would have to find a way.

If she even wanted to talk to me after what had happened today, of course.

I made my way down to the bar, and the bouncer let me in as soon as he saw the look on my face. He knew who I was, and he knew better than to try and stop me getting what I wanted. I was grateful. The last thing I needed right now was for someone to come in and cause me problems. I just wanted to get drunk and blow off some steam, and forget about the mess I had managed to make of my girlfriend's graduation day.

A bachelorette party was hanging over the bar, draped in shiny pink sashes and tiaras, and one of them locked on to me the moment she spotted me getting close.

"Oh, hey!" she squealed, as though she knew me. I had never seen her before in my life, but maybe some flirtation would get my head out of the mess it was in right now. I needed something to distract me from thinking about Amber, something to pull me back to reality.

"Hey," I replied, offering her a grin. She was a little younger than me, and I could tell from the look in her eyes she was already tipsy. All of them were hanging on to each other, talking over one another and laughing and shrieking. They must have been here for a while, drinking the night away, celebrating the impending nuptials of whichever one was going to get married.

"My best friend is getting married tomorrow," she told me, leaning in close, as though she was dropping some huge secret. I raised my eyebrows.

"Oh, yeah?"

"Yeah," she replied, batting her lashes at me. "Can you believe it?"

"I can't believe you'd come to a place like this to celebrate," I remarked, and I waved over the bartender and ordered them a bottle of champagne, along with a stay in the VIP section. I knew there was no good reason for me to do this, beyond getting a little attention from some cute girls, but I wanted to forget myself for now.

The women insisted I come with them to the VIP section and poured me a generous helping of champagne. I was already drunk enough, but I took it anyway, chugging away on the booze in the hopes it would be enough to take some of the edge off what I was feeling. I didn't know how long I could carry on like this, how long I could feel so lost without Amber, but I wanted to forget about her right now. She had walked out on me, and I wasn't going to go chasing after her. She had made it clear she wanted nothing to do with me, and I sure as hell wasn't going to go pushing her to give me something she didn't want to.

"You're so cute," the bride—what was her name, Anne?—cooed over me as she shuffled a little closer to me on the puffy leather chairs in the VIP section.

"He really is, isn't he?" added one of the other women. "And generous, too. You sure you're marrying the right guy, Anne?"

I smirked. I didn't know who her husband-to-be was, but I got the feeling he wouldn't have been too happy if he had caught wind of what I was doing here with his wife right now. Good. I felt like pissing some people off tonight. I had already made it so Amber didn't want to even look at me, why not make life a little harder for everyone else, too?

"I don't even know anymore," Anne sighed, tossing a thick hank of blond hair over one shoulder. "He's just...you're so handsome..."

She ran her fingers over my shoulder, and I wondered if I should make a move. Any other night, I would have had my arm around her already, pulling her in close to show her how interested I was, but I didn't know if I had it in me right now. Yeah, it would have served as a good distraction, but at the same time, it would have perma-fucked things with Amber. We'd had an argument, but that didn't mean I was in any rush to ruin the whole relationship because of it. Sometimes, people argued, and it didn't mean everything else had to be thrown away as a result. I pushed those thoughts down, trying to contain myself, even as the bride-to-be batted her lashes at me playfully.

I didn't want anyone but Amber. Even with this cute girl practically throwing herself at me, I couldn't have cared less. I wanted Amber to be here, for the two of us to sneak off to the bathroom like we had in the club the other night, unable to keep our hands off of each other. Even the thought of it was enough to make me smile. Being around her made everything else fall away.

But the closest thing I had to that tonight was drinking myself into a stupor, and I intended to do just that. I didn't want to think straight. I wanted to shut off the part of my brain telling me to go to her and get over it. She wanted her space? I would give it to her. I would give her all the space she wanted. When she was ready to talk, she could come to me, and we could discuss this like adults. Until then, though, I was going to keep drinking and do everything I could to forget she existed.

"What are you thinking about?" Anne asked me as she shifted a little closer to me on the seat. I shook my head. No way was I going to tell her I was pondering my actual girlfriend. It would have killed the mood, and I was still pretty sure I was in with a chance if I played my cards right.

"Nothing," I replied. "Let's get another drink."

"Who the fuck are you?"

A voice cut me off, and I looked up in surprise to see a man standing just outside the VIP section. He was glowering at me as though he wanted to rip my head off, and I knew before he so much as said a word who he was.

"Nathan, what are you doing here?" Anne exclaimed, leaping to her feet and away from me as though I had just burst into flames.

"Who the fuck is that?" her fiancé demanded, jabbing his finger in my direction. I bristled with annoyance. I hadn't done anything wrong. She was the one who was supposed to be getting married; it was on her to keep it in her pants. But now here he was, about to cause me some serious problems just for flirting with his would-be wife.

"You should go," I told him, getting to my feet to make my way over to him. He was swaying slightly, probably drunk himself, and I figured the best course of action would be to get him out of here. I might have been hammered in my own right, but I could handle myself when some pissed-off boyfriend turned up to cause trouble.

"You need to go!" he told me, stabbing his finger angrily in my direction. "What do you think you're doing here with my fiancée?"

Before I could duck, he swung a fist, and I just managed to get out of the way, but I tripped over the velvet rope separating the VIP section from the rest of the club in the process, nearly landing on my face. I managed to get myself upright a split-second before he swung for me again, and this time, he landed a blow on my chest, knocking me sideways. He was a heavy guy, and even in his inebriated state, he was strong.

I managed to pull myself upright, but before I could take a shot at him, one of the bouncers had jumped in to pull us apart. I could hear Anne yelling behind me, and a few of the girls with her trying to calm her down, but it was clear they were having a hard time.

"I'm going, I'm going," I muttered as one of the bouncers thrust me toward the door. I didn't need to be told twice. Hell, I wasn't sure I even wanted to be here in the first place. I was going to put as much distance between myself and this shithole as possible, if all I was going to get was trouble for turning up here. I didn't much feel like fighting to keep myself going when all I was doing was talking to a woman.

Fuck it. I needed to go home. I wanted to get some rest and work out what the hell I was going to do about the Amber situation. And then I could figure out how to get my girl back.

Because I wasn't going to let one bad day come between us. Not when I felt the way I did for her. And not when I was so certain she was the one for me.

Chapter Fourteen

Amber

I PUSHED OPEN THE DOOR and hurried in, planning to just grab my phone charger and get out. I'd left it here by accident when I had stormed out earlier, and I had driven all the way back across town to pick it up.

Or at least, that was what I was telling myself.

I was worried about Josh. When I had walked out earlier, I had left him to his own devices, and I knew he wasn't in a good place. He might have tried to lie and tell me he didn't give a damn, but I could see all of this was getting to him, even if he didn't want to admit it. He wanted to pretend he was bigger and badder than any kind of emotional pain that might come his way, but I knew him too well for that. This was the first real issue the two of us had ever had, and we both would have been lying if we said it wasn't kind of a nightmare to face our first problem like this, on a day that was supposed to be so special.

I couldn't stop thinking about the tickets I had seen on the table. Had he really been planning to take me to Hawaii? Nobody had ever taken me on a surprise trip before, and it blew my mind to think he would have put together something so major for us. Just for us, to enjoy a little time alone together, after everything that had happened. Maybe I should have given him some time to explain himself. It wasn't as though he was avoiding me, if he had something like this planned to whisk me away as soon as the graduation was over.

The apartment was quiet when I got there, and I looked around for Josh. He wasn't in bed, or on the balcony, so I had to guess he was out right now. Drinking? Probably. It seemed to be his go-to for handling anything he didn't like. I hoped he was okay.

I headed to the bedroom to grab my phone charger, and I was about to find some further excuse to stick around before I heard the front door open and the sound of footsteps staggering through the apartment. I heard a groan, and I hurried out to see what was going on.

It was Josh—he was back finally. He looked a little worse for wear, leaning heavily on the kitchen counter to keep himself upright. Even though I knew I should still be pissed at him, I hurried over to his side.

"Are you all right?" I asked him, concerned. "What's going on?"

"I'm fine," he muttered. He didn't seem at all surprised I was there, probably expected it, to some degree. He knew I wouldn't have been able to stay away from him for long. I was worried about him, even as I tried to keep my head clear. It was impossible to get him out of my mind.

His hair was a mess, and his face was covered with sweat. Whatever had happened, it wasn't good. I flicked on the light, and he winced in the glare.

"What happened to you?" I asked him as I popped open the drawer to pull out the first aid kit I knew was in there. I was certain he wouldn't want me fussing like this, but there was no way I was just going to stand back when he was hurt.

He didn't seem to have any visible injuries, but I mopped his brow and smoothed back his hair. He'd had too much to drink, that much was for sure, and I wondered where he had gone to keep the booze flowing. I wasn't even sure I wanted to know. I was just glad he was here, back with me, where he belonged. I wanted him beside me, even when we had been fighting, even when it was hard. I knew it wasn't always going to be easy when it came to our relationship, not with everything pulling in different directions at once, but I didn't care. I needed to be close to him. I needed this.

"You okay?" I murmured, and he nodded. He seemed glad I was there. He reached out to take my hand, bringing it to his lips and kissing the back of it gently. I closed my eyes. His sweetness always caught me off guard, even though I shouldn't have been surprised. He was just so kind to me sometimes, his softness coming out of a part of him I wasn't sure I would have believed was real if I hadn't seen it myself.

"Yeah, I'm okay," he replied. "And...I'm sorry. About what happened today. I know how important this was to you, and I don't want you to think I'm trying to get out of meeting your parents or taking this seriously."

I nodded. I was starting to believe it. Just because he hadn't exactly reacted the smartest way didn't mean he was out to hurt me. I knew he was trying to balance his family and me, and he was having a hard time navigating what a life looked like with both of us in it.

"I'm going to find a way to make this work," he promised me, clasping his hands around mine and looking at me intently. I wanted to believe him, I really did, and there was a part of me crying out to just lean over and kiss him and tell him I knew he could. I didn't want to say anything I couldn't take back, and I didn't want to put more pressure on him than I needed to. He was already dealing with enough shit as it was, and I didn't want him feeling like he had to rush to find some way to balance both sides of his life.

"And I promise, anything big like your graduation, I'm not going to miss it," he told me, his voice taking on an edge of certainty, like he wanted me to know how much he meant it. I believed him. Right now, at least. I knew I would have to wait and see if he actually followed through, but I believed him, I believed he would be there. Or at least, he would try.

I took a breath and glanced back over to the table where the tickets for the trip to Hawaii were still waiting. He hadn't brought them up, and I didn't want to assume anything. If I had pissed him off enough, he might have decided he didn't want to take the trip after all, and who could have blamed him?

"I saw the tickets on the table," I told him before I could stop myself. "Did you...did you plan a trip for us?"

A smile curled up his lips, and he nodded.

"Yeah, I did," he replied, sliding his hands to my waist. He looked a lot better now that I'd taken some care of him. Or maybe it was just because of the softness in his eyes when he looked at me, as though he was gazing at something he couldn't get enough of.

"Do you...do you still want to go?" I asked him, a little nervous. "I mean, I get it if you can't. I know your family needs you, and I don't want to get in the way of that..."

He cut me off with a kiss, pulling me in close, as though he didn't want to let me go.

"Baby, I wouldn't have booked that trip if I didn't want to take it with you," he pointed out, brushing his nose against mine. "Yes, I still want to go. I want to treat you to something special."

I smiled. I couldn't help it. I couldn't remember a time when someone had done something like this for me. Aaron had kept promising me that trip to Bali, but judging by how much he had been spending on his gambling addiction, I doubted he would have actually been able to do it. But Josh—Josh had seen the biggest achievement of my life so far, and he wanted to make sure we celebrated it in style.

"I actually have one more present I wanted to give you for your graduation," he murmured, and his eyes fell to my lips again. I could feel the heat starting to rise between us, and nothing I did could hold it back. I loved being with him like this, loved being close to him in this way. Even when we had issues, they never seemed insurmountable, not when he was around. He was still here, even despite our fight, willing to tell me he'd screwed up and that he wanted to work on it.

I closed my eyes and leaned forward to kiss him again. This time, the kiss came with a little more intensity, a little more purpose. I knew what I wanted from him, and I knew what he wanted from me, the desire coming off both of us in waves.

Even though I wasn't wearing the dress I had wanted to seduce him in, I still felt beautiful when he touched me, as though I was the most perfect creature he had ever laid eyes on. He smiled into the kiss, and I felt it all fall away—all the anger I had been dealing with, all the annoyance, it just seemed to vanish when his lips parted mine and he pushed his tongue deep inside to taste me properly.

He guided me back to the bedroom, and I wound my arms around him and pulled him on to the bed. I wanted to feel him inside me. I needed the promise that he was still here, just as he had been before our little fight. I wanted to make it up to him as best I could, to show him I was still here, and I still wanted and craved him with everything I had.

I wrapped my legs around him and kissed him harder, cupping his face in my hands. I could taste the booze on his tongue, but I didn't care. I wanted to get drunk on him, to gorge myself on how good it felt to be with him. He kissed down my neck, his breath hot on my skin as he stripped me out of the sweatpants and tee I'd worn down here. I hadn't been expecting to run into him, and certainly not like this, otherwise I would have dressed up.

But he still wanted me, no matter what state I was in. It didn't matter to him, and that turned me on beyond anything else. Knowing he wanted me, desired me, craved me no matter how I came to him was everything I wanted. His hands moved hungrily all over my body, stripping me down until I was utterly naked, and I groaned against his lips as he pushed his fingers between my legs to feel my aching pussy.

"Oh," I moaned helplessly, and he kissed me again, as though tasting the pleasure right from my mouth. He was hungry for me, his hardness already pressing against my thigh.

I knew I didn't want to wait any longer to feel him slide inside of me, and I spread my legs and arched my back, begging him to enter me. I wanted to feel his fullness buried deep inside of me; I wanted to lose myself to the feeling of the two of us coming together like this. I adored him. I adored him, and I didn't want to let one silly little argument get in the way of that.

He didn't need telling twice, guiding himself to the entrance of my pussy and then pressing himself against it. He slid inside of me in one long motion, and I sank back onto the bed as I allowed the pleasure to take me over. I couldn't think straight as he filled me, wrapping my arms around him and pulling him in as tightly as I could. I wanted to live in this moment forever, for as long as I could.

He began to move inside of me, taking his time at first, and then starting to pick up the pace a little. I reached down to grab on to his ass, pulling him deeper and deeper, letting him take me. I needed this. I turned my head to kiss him again, pushing my tongue into his mouth so I could taste him properly. I was addicted to the way it felt, to the way he made me feel, and I didn't want to lose it. I didn't want to miss an instant of it.

"Fuck, you feel so good," he groaned in my ear, and hearing how turned on he was by this was enough to inch me closer and closer to the edge. I could feel myself starting to crest, the pleasure beginning to get the better of me, and I didn't want this moment to end.

My breath was starting to come harder and faster out of my throat, and the pressure was beginning to inch toward impossible levels. I couldn't hold back, even if I wanted to, the pleasure starting to get the better of me until finally, I felt it give in, the orgasm exploding through me in an intense rush that made me cry out with relief.

I squeezed my thighs around him, holding him there as he pushed deep inside of me and didn't move, letting my pussy massage him from the inside out. The pleasure was almost impossible, too much for me to make sense of, and it seemed like my entire body was giving in as I let myself go, let myself sink in to the delicious sensations he was sending coursing through every one of my nerve endings.

It didn't take long till he, too, tipped over the edge and into his own release, filling me with his seed, holding himself there for a long moment before he slowly pulled out again. His body was tense, but his kiss was soft as his lips found mine once more. I cupped his head in my hands, holding him there, just looking up at him with so much love it almost hurt.

I wanted to say it to him, to drop those words, but I didn't want to rush it. I didn't want this to go any quicker than it already had. I knew how he felt about me—he had already made that as clear as he could—and all that mattered was that he was here, in bed with me, showing me how much he wanted me.

Oh, and those tickets to Hawaii, too. Those were pretty damn good as well.

Chapter Fifteen

Josh

AS I STOOD OUTSIDE my father's door, I tried to pull myself together. I knew there was so much I wanted to say to him, but I wasn't certain how he would take any of it.

If I had learned one thing in getting a little more involved with the family business, it was that my father didn't like feeling as though he was second on someone's list of priorities. No matter how much I tried to convince him I was committed to this, he was going to think I was trying to get out of my duties. I just had to hope he would accept this as payment for all the work I had been doing for the family business in the last few weeks, even if it hadn't come at the best time.

Amber had already gotten herself totally excited about the thought of a trip to Hawaii, and I didn't want to let her down. She deserved a break after all she had been through, and I wasn't going to fail on this front. She had seen the tickets, and I couldn't wait to sweep her off on a romantic trip for just the two of us. It was my way of making up for how badly I had flaked at her graduation, and she seemed willing to put all of it behind her if we could just spend a little more time together, away from the intensity of all of this.

I pushed open my father's office door, knowing I was going to have to make a good case for myself here. He liked Amber well enough, but that didn't mean he would be in any rush to let us get out of the country, out of work for a little while. Honestly, I had been craving it badly, knowing I needed a break before something snapped. Working this hard, dedicating so much of my life to clearing up my father's messes and handling our family business, had taken a lot out of me.

My father looked up as soon as he heard me come in and offered me a smile in greeting. I was still getting used to him meeting me with friendliness instead of a frown. I had been letting him down for so long, it had become almost normal to me to see him sigh when I walked into a room.

"Afternoon," he greeted me.

I nodded back. "Can we talk?"

A brief cloud passed over his face, and I could tell he was worried I was going to come out with something he wasn't going to enjoy. I wished I could get it through to him, make him understand I was in this now, and I didn't intend to fuck up like I had before. Yes, the two of us hadn't always had it easy, but I was going to change that. I would put in the work to make it happen. I felt like I had already.

"Yes, of course," he replied, and he gestured to the seat opposite him. "Please, sit down."

I took a seat carefully, trying to play this as calmly as I could. I didn't want him to freak out about me going on vacation. I knew it was going to be tough for him to hear I was leaving, but hopefully he would understand this was a chance for me to make sure my relationship with Amber was on the right track. He clearly wanted me to settle down with her, and I intended to do all I could to make it happen. We had something special, and I wanted to show her I saw that.

"I'd like to take some time away," I explained. "From the city. Just a week or so, with Amber. I want to take her to Hawaii to celebrate her graduation."

He eyed me for a moment and then leaned back in his seat before he responded. I could see the glint in his eye, and I could tell there was something bigger on his mind, something better.

"I have a counter-offer," he replied.

"Which is?"

"How about a trip to Italy?"

I raised my eyebrows at him. "You're offering me a trip?"

"Well, it's for work," he explained. "But there'll be plenty of time to spend with your woman while you're there. It's a beautiful part of the world. Plenty of shopping to keep her busy, too."

I didn't contradict him, though I was sure Amber would have. She had interests outside of shopping. I knew there was no point trying to get my old-fashioned father to see it any differently, though. He had his mind made up, and not much would have changed it.

"I'll pay you while you're out there," he explained. "Tommy'll go with you. I have a job for you."

I raised my eyebrows. A job? I couldn't imagine what kind of job would require me to go all the way to Europe, but my father wouldn't have offered unless it was something good.

"What kind of job?"

"I have a contact out there, Silvio," he explained, leaning forward. "The two of us have been in touch a little over the last few weeks. He's got an idea he wants to pull me in on, and frankly, I think it's a good one."

"Which is?"

"Match-fixing in *Serie A,*" he explained. "The soccer league out there. There's good money in it, and they're all corrupt as they come anyway."

"And what about if something goes wrong?" I asked him. "They take soccer pretty seriously out there, they're not going to take it well—"

"That's where Silvio comes in," he cut in. "He's willing to take the fall—if it comes to that—as long as I put up the capital for this venture. Works for me. Makes sense."

I nodded. Honestly, I could see why it would be a good idea, but at the same time, I was concerned about how it would go down. What if it went wrong? Would this Silvio guy really cover for my father, or would he sell him down the river the first chance he got? There was no way for us to know for sure, and my father couldn't have been absolutely certain no matter how much he wanted to.

"I think I can trust him, but it's why I want to send you and Tommy down to get a feel for him," he explained. "The two of you have good instincts; you'll be able to tell if this guy is trying to fuck me around. I trust both of you."

I nodded again. Honestly, I knew this was a big deal for him, putting me on the same pedestal as Tommy. Normally, I knew my brother would have been the only one going out there, the only one my father actually trusted to handle all of this, but the way he was talking, it was clear he believed I would bring something to the table, too. I mean, none of this was how I had pictured spending my time with Amber now that she had graduated, but maybe I could spin it in a way that would make her feel she was getting the better deal. Italy was certainly farther away than Hawaii, a bigger adventure for both of us.

I was going to do it. I knew I couldn't pass up the chance to impress my father. And this was a way for me to take her out of the country without compromising how far things had come with my family. All in all, it was as win-win, and I knew I needed to see it that way. It might have been a change of plans, but it was entirely for the better, and I wasn't going to miss the chance to do it.

"I'll go," I replied, and a smile cracked wide over my father's face. I was glad to see it there. I wanted nothing more than to please him, to make sure he knew I was really committed to the family. I hadn't always been there, but I was never going to go back to what I had been doing before and fail them again. They deserved my help. After everything they had done for me, it seemed the least I could offer in return.

Dad grinned, reaching across the table to put a hand on my shoulder. As he looked at me, I felt something twinge in my chest. It had been a long time since he had gazed at me like he was in any way proud of me, like he was really glad I was here. I had fucked up too many times for that. But here, in this moment, it was like everything else just dropped away. I could finally be the son he wanted me to be, the one he had been pushing for this whole time. My mind flashed back briefly to the way he had hurt me in this very office, and I pushed it down. It wasn't going to happen again. I was never going to give him a reason to hurt me like that again.

"Good man," he told me, and he leaned back in his seat. "I'll get everything booked for you. You tell your girl that you're taking her to Italy."

I got to my feet. "I will."

I headed back to my place, where Amber was waiting for me. I hadn't told her what I was planning to speak to my father about, but at least I had some good news to share with her. I wanted to make sure she saw this as a good thing, even if we were changing our plans a little. I was sure she would go along with it. The way she had been acting since the night before, after we had kissed and made up, told me she would have pretty much agreed with anything I offered her right now.

"I have some good news," I told her as I kissed her in greeting. She wound her arms around me and looked at me curiously, her eyes lighting up.

"Oh, yeah?"

"We're not going to Hawaii," I explained. "We're going to Italy instead."

Her eyes widened, her lips parting in shock. "Italy?" she squealed.

"Yeah, Italy," I replied. "Sound good?"

"Oh my goodness, Josh," she blurted out, shaking her head. "I—you didn't have to go this far..."

I grinned, planting a kiss on her lips. I just wanted her to have everything that was coming to her. She deserved it more than anyone I had ever met before in my life. Her kindness, her sweetness, her honesty, she deserved the world at her feet, and if the best I could give her right now was Italy, I would do it.

"We'll do Hawaii some other time," I promised her. "But this sounds like a whole lot more fun."

"I've never even left the country before," she murmured as it all sank in. "Am I going to have to learn Italian? Oh, I need to start practicing right away..."

I grinned as she hurried off to grab her phone, downloading an app that she could use to learn a little more of the language. I loved seeing her this excited. I'd always wanted to be able to give her this kind of joy. If I had to take her around the world, to every damn country to make sure it happened, I would.

I wanted to bring her all the joy in the world. She deserved it. Because when I looked at her, I saw someone I wanted to spend my life with—someone I wanted to give this sort of happiness to at every turn. I knew it might not last forever, but right now, it seemed impossible that it could ever end.

Chapter Sixteen

Amber

I STILL COULDN'T BELIEVE the trip we would be on in just a couple of days.

I had been happy enough with a visit to Hawaii—hell, I had been beyond excited at the thought of taking a few days to recline on some white-sand beach to relax and chill out—but now, I was heading to one of my dream vacation spots, a place I thought I'd have to save up for years to even get close to. I didn't know what had caused Josh's chance of heart, but with a trip to Italy waiting for me, there was no way in hell I was going to argue.

I had been packing my stuff all weekend, getting everything together so I was ready to leave when our taxi arrived to sweep us off to the airport. I had been practicing my Italian, what little of it I had, so I wouldn't make a total fool of myself when I got there, but Josh had been telling me everyone would likely speak English, anyway.

"You don't need to worry about speaking the language," he had tried to assure me, and I shook my head.

"I'm not going to be one of those Americans who walks around thinking it's all going to revolve around her," I replied.

"Why not?" he remarked with a grin, wrapping his arms around me. "As long as I'm there, it will."

And he had proved that to be the case at every turn. He'd picked me up a set of Gucci luggage to travel with, and I was still getting over how gorgeous it was. I had never owned anything this expensive in my life, and he had given it to me like it was nothing.

"You deserve it," he told me with a shrug. "A little something for your graduation."

I wasn't going to argue with him. I was still trying to get used to this new lifestyle that he came with, even though I knew I had to run with it. All the luxury, all the glamor, it was almost more than I could wrap my head around, but there was no way I was going to deny myself. Aaron had talked a big game about treating me right, but it was nothing in comparison to the way Josh handled our relationship. He showered me with attention, with gifts, with sweetness like it was the most natural thing in the world.

I could get used to it, I really could. I loved knowing I was the center of his attention. Maybe it was a little selfish, but after being fucked around for so long, to have a guy who was utterly dedicated to me was a thrill. He didn't want anything or anyone other than me, and I loved the way it made me feel. Totally secure, totally sure of myself, like nothing could have moved me from the path.

It was just a matter of days until we left, and he was making sure everything was ready for us when we got out of the country. I had let my parents know I was going to be traveling for a little while, and my mother had sounded beyond shocked.

"What about your career?" she asked. "Don't you want to get out there and start looking for jobs?"

"I will when I get back," I promised her, and I meant it. As much fun as it was to indulge myself in the thrill of everything happening around me, I didn't want to rely on him for the rest of my life. I had worked too hard to get where I was, too hard to graduate with a useful degree, and I wasn't going to just forget about all of it to become some pampered stay-at-home girlfriend.

Though really, the thought of it was tempting right now. All the romance he had treated me to, all the gifts and sweetness were enough to get me wondering if I had made the right choice pursuing a career. I knew he would have showered me with anything I asked for, taken care of me in every way he was able to, but I wanted to have a life of my own. I needed to. I didn't want him to resent me for taking from him, after all. When he had met me, I had my own life, and it was important I kept that up now we were really together.

But I could put it to the back of my mind for now, because we were going across the world together on a gorgeous trip I could hardly wait for. I knew there had to be some reason for his change of plans, after he had invested so much time into getting those tickets to Hawaii, but I was trying not to think about it. If he had to work a little while we were there, I could handle it. It didn't have to be some big deal, something for me to get all hung up about.

Tommy was going too, though I imagined he would do what he could to keep out of our way. Josh had casually referred to it as our honeymoon, and honestly, I couldn't stop thinking about it in those terms. It was exactly how I wanted to see it, a chance for us to show how much we cared about each other and how hard we were falling for each other. A million times better than the stilted, awkward, awful trip to Bali I was going to take for my actual honeymoon.

I couldn't get over how different things felt with Josh than with Aaron. I couldn't believe I had really been planning to *marry* that man, when I could look back now and see there was no way I even really cared about him. I liked him well enough, at least at the start, but the more time that passed, the more and more certain I should have become that we couldn't make it work. I wanted to believe I could, but I had had one foot out the door even before I met Josh. He had just been the little push it took to get me over the edge and into what I needed to do.

But I was here now, I had made the choice, and nothing would have convinced me to undo it. I was falling for him. I was probably already in love with him, but I didn't know if I was ready to say it yet. It had all happened so quickly, and I didn't want to freak him out by coming on too strong, even if it was how I genuinely felt.

A trip away would do us good, a chance for us to clear our heads and focus on each other. I couldn't wait to have him all to myself for a while. I had been looking up everything I could about the place we were staying, a little village on the coast not far from Sicily and was finding myself more and more excited with every moment that passed.

I had just about finished packing all my clothes for the trip when Josh wandered into the bedroom, eyeing the luggage I had splayed out all over the bed.

"You think you've got enough?" he joked playfully, sliding his arms around my waist from behind and pulling me in close.

"I think I'm getting there," I replied, turning to plant a kiss on his cheek.

"Have you got room for something else?" he asked, pulling away from me and reaching into his pocket. I raised my eyebrows at him. Had he really just gotten me something else?

"Like what?"

"Nothing big," he replied, and he handed me a small oval container from his pocket. I glanced up at him and then popped it open—and gasped when I saw the diamond-encrusted sunglasses inside.

"Josh, what the hell?" I exclaimed. Like he hadn't gotten enough for me as it was. Did he have any idea when to stop? Clearly, he wanted to indulge me every chance he got, and I wasn't going to go complaining.

"I thought you could use a new pair," he replied with a playful grin. "Do you like them?"

"I love them," I replied, lifting them almost reverently from the case and slipping them on my face. I glanced at myself in the mirror, and honestly, it took me a moment to recognize myself. I seemed so...just so *different* from the person I had been before. I would never have been able to afford these, and Aaron would never have thought to treat me to something so luxurious. But Josh saw this stuff and decided I deserved it. It was going to take me a while to get used to it, but I didn't intend on complaining.

"Thank you," I told him, and I pulled off the sunglasses and kissed him again. I couldn't wrap my head around how much he indulged me, how much he wanted to show the way he cared for me. I adored him, I really did, and I wanted to do what I could to make sure he understood that.

I moved my hand to the waistband of his jeans, grazing my fingers over the top, and then dropped to my knees in front of him. His eyebrow cocked as he looked down at me, but he didn't make a move to stop me.

"Can I show you how grateful I am?" I cooed as I toyed with his zipper.

"Go right ahead," he murmured as he pushed my hair back from my face and cupped my chin so I was looking up at him. I adored the way he gazed at me, as though he really couldn't believe I was all his, but I was. I loved this, loved being able to give him something in return for all he had gifted me.

I unzipped his pants, pushed down his boxers, and pulled his now-hard cock into my hand, stroking it a couple of times to make sure he was totally erect. He really did have the most perfect dick I had ever seen. I bit my lip as I gazed up at him, making sure he knew how much I wanted this, wanted him. He had indulged me in all the ways he could think of, and I wanted to give a little back, make sure he knew just how much I appreciated it.

I parted my lips and closed my eyes, leaning forward to swirl my tongue around the head of his cock. I could already taste a drop of pre-cum there, a delicious little promise of what was to come. I moaned slightly, and I heard him growl with desire above me, clearly wanting as much as he could take. He moved his hips forward slightly, sliding a couple of inches of his cock into my mouth, and I sucked on his tip, letting him feel the pressure starting to build. Sliding my hands to his thighs, I pulled him in closer.

I felt him slide a little farther into my mouth, and I couldn't resist slipping my hand between my legs to play with myself as I took his cock between my lips. He just tasted so damn good, I couldn't resist it. There was something so erotic about pleasuring him like this, knowing I was in total control of the situation and that he was giving in to the way I was making him feel. I wasn't sure I would ever get tired of it.

I massaged my clit as I drew him deeper into my mouth, sealing my lips around him and beginning to bob my head back and forth. I could feel him starting to get even stiffer in my mouth, and I took it as the sign I needed to move a little faster, apply a little more pressure.

He groaned loudly, and I looked up, stealing a glance at him as I pleasured him with my lips and tongue. His head was tilted back, his jaw tense, his body totally given over to the pleasure I was gifting to him, and I loved it. Loved seeing him like this, watching him give in to the way I could make him feel.

My fingers moved a little quicker between my legs, and I clamped my thighs together as I began to work my tongue along the underside of his cock. I wanted him to come in my mouth. I wanted to taste him.

He looked down at me, his hand brushing over my hair as he watched me go down on him. His skin was velvety-smooth and tasted utterly and deliciously of him. I wanted to gorge myself on this flavor, make it so there was no room for anything else but him, the way he tasted, the way he made me feel.

"Fuck, you look so good like that," he moaned, and the sound of his voice sent a cascade of pleasure through my whole system. I began to move a little more quickly, needing this, needing to feel him finish in my mouth. I wanted to be enough for him, for the sight of me like this to be enough to take him over the edge and into the release he needed so badly.

He pushed himself deep into my mouth and held himself there, and a few seconds later, I felt his cock twitch as he finished. The feeling as he came was almost more than I could take, the arousal taking control of me as I moaned against him. My fingers were practically a blur between my legs, and a few seconds after he reached his release, I finished myself, the orgasm finally softening the edges of the desperate want consuming me.

Once he had finished, he slowly slipped back, catching his breath, and I sat back on my heels and gazed up at him happily. I loved knowing how much I turned him on, how even the sight of me going down on him was enough to make it impossible for him to think straight.

"How are you so good at that?" he murmured as he pulled me back to my feet, nuzzling into my neck. I grinned.

"I don't know," I admitted. "But I think I could use a whole lot more practice..."

Chapter Seventeen

Amber

I STEPPED BACK, CASTING one more look over everything I had packed for the trip. I was pretty sure I was ready to go, and I wanted nothing more than to get on that flight and go to Italy at last.

It had only been a couple of days since Josh had told me he was going to take me across the world, but I had been itching with excitement ever since. I couldn't wait to travel with him. The two of us together in a foreign country...it was going to be so much fun. I could hardly wait.

Well, not just the two of us, of course. Tommy was going to be there too. I was hoping his brother would be able to make it so Josh didn't have to spend the whole trip distracted with work. I wanted him to myself at least some of the time, even though I knew I was probably being greedy.

I didn't mind his brother being there, as long as it didn't get in the way of any of the fun Josh and I were planning on having together. Tommy and I got along well enough, but I didn't really know him, and I wasn't sure what he thought about me yet. He seemed cautious, as though all too aware that one wrong move might make it even harder for Josh than it already had been. I had walked into his life at a really strange time, just as his father had been caught up in a major health crisis, and I couldn't blame him for being distracted.

I hoped I would get a chance to know him better on this trip, though. It was clear he was an important part of Josh's life, and I didn't want anything to come between them, least of all me. I knew how intense relationships could be between twins, let alone when those twins were part of a criminal empire.

Honestly, it was a little strange being around Tommy. Sometimes he looked so much like Josh I would find myself getting a bit freaked, seeing Josh's beautiful blue eyes replaced by Tommy's dark brown ones. They were both gorgeous men, no doubt about it, and if I had met Tommy in a different circumstance, maybe I would have gone after him instead.

I supposed I wasn't the first woman to think that about a pair of brothers who looked so alike. Spending time with Tommy, I had noticed he seemed a little more level-headed than Josh, a little calmer, like he knew how important it was to come across as mature and cool. Josh was clearly different, more passionate, more driven, and I loved that about him, but I was curious to see how it worked with Tommy as well.

There was a knock on the bedroom door, and I turned, surprised. Josh never bothered with a knock, not in his own place. I turned, and, to my shock, I saw Tommy standing there. I wasn't sure the two of us had ever been alone together, and I would have been lying if I said I wasn't a little thrown by it.

"Oh, hey," I greeted him, straightening up slightly, hoping I didn't look too surprised by his arrival.

"Hi," he replied. "You're a lawyer, right?"

"Uh, I graduated from law school," I offered, furrowing my brow, not entirely sure what he was getting at. He had never really talked to me about my career before, and I was surprised he even remembered what it was.

"I have some contracts I'd like someone to look over, but our usual guy is busy till the end of the week," he explained, jerking his head back toward the door. "Josh said you would be here. You mind taking a look at them for me?"

"No, not at all," I replied immediately. I was glad I could actually be of some use to them for a change. I often felt as though I was just hanging on for dear life to their coat-tails, and I was willing to do whatever I could to prove differently, even just to myself.

"I have them laid out on the table," he explained, gesturing for me to come through, and I followed him. It was quiet in the apartment, and I couldn't help but notice it. I wanted to say something, but I didn't know what.

"Here they are," he told me, gesturing to a stack of papers on the table in front of me. I took a seat and pulled them toward me, looking them over.

I wasn't sure what I was expecting, but they seemed all right to me. I wasn't an expert in contract law by any stretch of the imagination, but I couldn't see anything jumping out at me to tell me there was a major problem. I took my time going over them, trying to ignore Tommy pacing beside me. There was something about being around him without Josh there between us that felt...strange. In a way I couldn't put my finger on.

"They look pretty good to me," I told him once I was done. I was flattered he had thought to come to me for help with this in the first place, to be honest, and I hoped I hadn't fucked this up. I wanted him to feel like he could come to me if they needed help in future.

"Did you do them yourself?" I asked, and as I looked up at him, I froze on the spot. He was looking at me. And I mean, *really* looking at me. His eyes were resting on my cleavage, his teeth on his bottom lip, as though there was something on his mind he knew he couldn't have said out loud.

"Hmm?" he replied as though distracted. I squirmed in my chair. Why was he looking at me like that? Why did I not hate it as much as I should? I told myself it was just because he looked so much like Josh I was letting myself believe it was no different.

"Yeah, I did," he added once it clicked with him what I was asking. How long had he been distracted by my body like that? And why didn't I mind?

"They're good," I replied, hoping to keep the slight shock out of my voice. I didn't want him thinking I had noticed his attraction to me. I wasn't sure if it would have been a bad thing or not for me to notice. How long had he been looking at me like that? Had I just been distracted enough by Josh not to notice?

He was still looking at me with that expression on his face, as though there was something he wanted to say but wasn't quite sure how to come out with it. I swallowed. I knew I wasn't going to call him out on it, not a chance in hell. It would have been crazy to even consider it. And yet—and yet, there was a part of me that wanted to tell him I had seen him staring at me. Seen him wanting me.

How hard up was he that he was eyeing his brother's girl? I had no idea. He had never mentioned anyone to me in the past, and I figured he was as single as they came. But still, I would have been lying if I said I didn't enjoy the attention a little. The tension between us was there, impossible to deny, and I knew there was no way for me to pretend I didn't see it. I liked it. A lot.

Maybe the attraction was a little more mutual than I would have cared to admit. I didn't know what to say to him, the silence hanging in the air between us, as though neither of us could put it into words. I should have left, gotten out of there so I could get back to what I had been doing, but I wanted to keep lingering here a little longer.

"You're coming with us to Italy, right?" I asked him, and he nodded.

"Yeah, I am."

"Have you been before?"

"Once, when I was a lot younger," he replied. "It's a beautiful country. You'll love it."

"I know I will," I agreed, unable to keep the smile off my face. "I...it's going to be so much fun."

"Yeah, it will," he replied. I flicked my tongue over my bottom lip. There was more I wanted to say to him—maybe even some intention of calling him out on the way he had been looking at me—but I didn't have anything close to the nerve to do it right now. Better to push it down. Whatever had happened was over now, and I wasn't going to let it turn into some big, crazy thing I needed to address.

"Good chance for us to spend some time together, too," he remarked, leaning forward slightly, a smile on his lips. Damn, he really was hot. I still thought Josh was the sexier of the two, but his twin had a certain something to him as well. I had never really allowed myself to just look at him the way I was now, but I was enjoying it. Enjoying the tension between us, the way he seemed unable to take his eyes off me. Was this wrong? Probably. But people got crushes sometimes, didn't they? It didn't mean it had to turn into anything. It was just a little fun flirtation, a way for us to deal with the stress of our lives.

He was going to be around a lot while we were in Italy. He'd probably see me in my bikini. I could almost picture the way he would stare at me, the obvious appreciation in his eyes. Would Josh notice it, too? How would he react? I had no idea, but I didn't intend to find out, not if I could avoid it. I didn't need to be causing any more problems in this family. I needed to keep my head down and remember which brother I was actually with before I let some stupid crush get the better of me.

"Thanks for your help," he told me as he gathered up the papers. I shrugged.

"Anytime," I replied. "I like feeling as though I can actually help out."

"Oh, I'm sure there's plenty you can do to make yourself useful," he replied, his eyes flashing with amusement. I felt a heat in my chest again and tried to ignore it. No way was I going to let this get to me. A little crush, that was all it was, and given I was dating an identical twin, how could it come as a surprise?

He headed out of the apartment, and I let out a breath I didn't even realize I had been holding. Okay. I could do this. We left for the trip in a couple of days, and when we did, I was going to have done everything I could to put whatever this was behind me.

Once and for all.

Chapter Eighteen

Josh

AS I DRAPED MY ARM over the back of her seat, Amber turned to me and smiled. The rays of the setting sun before us glowed on her face, lighting her up and making her look as though she had come from another planet entirely. Sometimes, I felt like she had—someone outside the family, who seemed so self-assured in the person they were and who they wanted to be.

"What do you think?" I asked. The sea air blew in gently around us, ruffling her hair, and she sighed happily.

"I think it's gorgeous," she replied. "And I bet it's going to be even more gorgeous when I get over this jetlag."

I grinned. She was right. It was our first evening here in Italy, and though we were both tired, it was stunning. The hotel we were staying in led to a private beach where we were watching the sunset together, just the two of us. It honestly felt like we might be the only people in the whole world.

Tommy was back at the hotel, getting everything set up for our meetings the next day, but for now, it was just Amber and me. I knew we wouldn't have a huge amount of time to just spend together, and I wanted to make the most of it. I loved being here with her, I really did. I loved knowing the two of us were really starting to settle into being a true couple, taking trips together, sharing our lives together.

I could get used to it, for sure. Having her with me all the time. She looked so beautiful with the warm golden rays of the setting sun playing on her face, and I wanted to capture this moment in my mind forever.

I couldn't believe how right it felt, being here with her, knowing we were taking this huge trip together. She had left everything behind to be with me, and I was so touched she wanted to come to this new country with me on a whim. Yeah, she had said it was a dream destination for her, but I was still a little surprised she had agreed to it. We had only been together a couple of months, but she was already so sure she wanted to be part of my life, even the parts of it I wouldn't have shown to other people.

She snuggled against my shoulder and bit back a yawn.

"You tired?" I asked.

"Yeah, but I'm not ready to go back to the hotel yet," she replied. "I want to drink all of this in. I don't want to miss a thing."

I pressed my lips into her hair, smiling as I listened to her speak. She was so in the moment, always focused on enjoying things in any way she could. I needed to take a lesson or two from her, try to do the same. I was already thinking about what I was going to need to do to take care of work tomorrow and for the following few weeks, even though Tommy had told me he would cover as much of it as he could for the time being. He knew I wanted to spend all the time I could with Amber, to make the most of our time together while we could enjoy it. It might not have been exactly how I wanted our first vacation together to go, but hey, I would take anything I could get. I was able to treat her to a trip away and make sure I didn't piss off my father in the process, too. That had to count for something, didn't it?

"Yeah, me too," I agreed, and I closed my eyes and inhaled the scent of her hair. I was really here, with her, away from the hustle and bustle of life back home. It wouldn't last forever. But as long as I had her here, as long as the two of us were together, I could make anything work. When she was around, everything seemed to click into place, like this was what my life had been waiting for.

"So what do you want to do now we're here?" she asked, and I sighed.

"Well, I'm going to have to deal with work," I reminded her. "Not ideal, I know, but I'll make it as quick as I can."

"That's okay," she replied, and she hesitated a moment. "You know, Tommy got me to look over some contracts for him before we left," she remarked casually. I hadn't heard anything of this. What was she talking about?

"Oh, yeah?" I replied. I had done my best to keep her out of the family business, but clearly, my brother didn't have the same qualms.

"Yeah," she replied.

"And how do you feel about it?" I asked. "Helping out with the family business, I mean."

"I didn't mind," she replied. "I'm glad I could do something to make a difference, you know? I don't want you to feel as though I'm just along for the ride."

"I never did," I assured her, and she smiled at me, a little nervous.

"Well, it was fine," she told me. "And I was glad I could use my degree for something. I need to keep my skills sharp if I want to get back to working soon."

"I guess you do," I agreed, leaning back on the bench behind us. "You want to work with us?" I added, and she peered over at me, obviously surprised.

"On...on the business?"

"We can, if you want," I replied. "It would mean more trips like this. But it would also mean working more closely with my father. And you know what his line of business is. It's not for everyone."

She paused for a moment, pondering the possibility. It was clear it was the first time she had really given it any serious thought. I wasn't sure what I wanted her to say.

"What's the other option?" she asked. "If I don't want to do that, I mean?"

"We could...we could get out together," I offered her. It was something I had pondered a little. I didn't have to commit the rest of my life to my father's business if I didn't want to. Sure, it wasn't going to go down well if I wanted to take a break from it, but at the same time, there was a whole life out there I had never experienced. A normal one. One built around just having fun, being with the women I loved, relaxing, and focusing on my passions and what I really cared about outside of the family business. I knew it might have been difficult to convince my father there was more to life than what he had built, but if I tried, I knew I could find a way to pull it off.

She fell silent for a moment. It was clear she had never considered the possibility of the two of us striking out on our own to make a new life together, but she wasn't brushing it off. She must have known she wouldn't have the same opportunities if we did that. We wouldn't be able to take trips like this one at the drop of a hat anymore. But maybe she would be okay with it. It was hard for me to believe sometimes that someone like her could really want me for more than what I could offer her, but she had shown me time and time again how much she valued me as a person, too.

"I honestly don't know which I prefer," she admitted. "I'll need some time to think about it."

"Well, you have all the time you need on this trip," I remarked, gesturing to the sea in front of us. Even the air smelled different here, as though everything was starting over fresh. I loved it. I couldn't get enough.

"Yeah, I'm going to take some time and go over what I think the best call is," she agreed, turning to smile at me. "Is that okay?"

"Of course it is," I replied, and I took her hand and brought it to my lips, pressing a kiss against her palm. I inhaled the scent of her skin, unable to get enough of it. It didn't matter how much time I spent with her, I was always craving more, always needed some little taste of her whenever I got the chance.

"I can't believe we're really here," she murmured as she turned to look back out over the sea before us.

"Me neither," I agreed.

"I just...I'm so grateful," she told me, as she snuggled in closer to me. "I never would have gotten a chance to do something like this if it hadn't been for you, and I need you to know how much I appreciate it. Honestly. I don't think I'll ever get over it."

I smiled. I loved hearing her happy. It made my chest tighten in the best way possible, like the world was trying to remind me why I was with her in the first place.

"I'm glad," I murmured back. "I'm just happy you're here with me, too."

"I don't want this to end," she continued, her voice taking on an emotional edge. "I just...it feels so right, you know? Being here with you. Somewhere new. Getting to explore this with you."

I grinned a little wider. The way she was talking, she was making it hard for me to think straight. When I was around her, when she was gushing about me and our relationship the way she was, I just wanted to gift her the whole world in a bow. She deserved it. She deserved everything.

"You keep talking like that," I warned her, "and you're going to be Mrs. Falcone by the time you leave."

I felt her shift a little closer to me, letting her hand rest on my leg playfully.

"Maybe it wouldn't be such a bad thing," she suggested. It was the first time we had actually spoken about marriage in such brazen terms, and knowing she wasn't exactly opposed to it was a huge relief.

Whatever the rest of the trip bought, this first night was perfect, and I didn't want to lose a second of it. I wanted to remember every little detail with her.

And I wasn't going to miss a damn thing.

Chapter Nineteen

Amber

WE WALKED HAND IN HAND back up toward the beautiful boutique hotel we were staying in while we were in Italy, and honestly, I felt as though I was strolling on air.

I couldn't believe we were really here. The trip had been long, and I was still getting used to being on foreign soil for the first time, but the excitement was enough to carry me through. I just loved being here with him. Loved spending time with him in this almost absurdly romantic setting.

And now he was talking about marrying me? I knew it was quick, but it felt so right, too. It felt like we had been destined for this since the moment we had met. To think, I had been engaged to someone else and trying to fool myself into thinking there was someone other than him out there for me when I knew I should have been his from the start.

He squeezed my hand as though all the same thoughts were running through his head. I tried to bite back another yawn, but the jetlag was getting the better of me. I got crotchety when I hadn't slept, and I didn't want to do something to ruin this perfect little moment between us.

The hotel we were staying at was gorgeous, and our rooms were already set up for us. We had dropped our luggage earlier, and they had told us they would bring it to our hotel room so we could relax for the rest of the evening. Tommy had headed down to a local bar, and I was more than happy to let him blow off some steam.

I couldn't stop thinking about the way he had looked at me when we had been alone together in the apartment. I knew I should have been able to get it out of my head, but there was something about it, something sexy and enticing I couldn't quite deny. I had been doing my best to shake it, and I hoped Josh hadn't worked out what was going on. The last thing I wanted was for him to start feeling jealous of his brother, especially when all three of us were going to be spending so much time together in the near future.

We arrived at reception to pick up our room keys, and a beautiful woman smiled at us in greeting. I shriveled into myself a little. She was a knockout; she looked like she belonged on a runway or something, not behind a hotel desk. Her long blond hair flowed over her shoulders, her eyes bright blue and sharp, her cheekbones so high I was pretty sure I could have skied off them.

"Mr. Falcone," she greeted Josh, her eyes sliding right over to him as though I wasn't standing there at all. I tried not to let it get to me. I had to understand this was part of the culture; people spoke to the men first. The women were there as not much more than decoration even though I was sure there was more I could do.

"Carina," he replied. How did he know her name? Had he spoken to her before? She flashed him a dazzling smile and reached beneath the desk to pull out our key cards, handing them both to Josh. Hello? Did she see me here at all? I was standing right beside him, but the way she was acting, it was like I was invisible.

"Your room is ready," she told him. "Would you like me to show you up?"

"That would be great," Josh replied, and I bristled. This place wasn't that big, and I wanted to be rid of this woman sooner rather than later. I didn't like the thought of her hanging around. I got it, she worked here, she was just doing her job, but as she led Josh to the stairs and practically forced me to follow behind the two of them, I wondered if she realized how bad this made her look.

Maybe she was hoping to get Josh for herself. I mean, she didn't stand a chance, but it bugged me that he didn't seem more focused on me right now. After everything that had happened with Aaron, I was a little more paranoid than I would have been before. I knew it wasn't Josh's fault I had been cheated on, and that it had happened with my best friend, of all people, but I didn't like feeling as though his attention was focused on another woman, especially one who seemed to be flirting with him.

I grabbed his hand as we made our way up the stairs, catching up to him to make sure he didn't get away from me. He glanced over and raised his eyebrows, silently asking just what I was doing. Maybe it was just the jetlag, but I didn't like being treated like this. I didn't want to ruin our first night here, but I wasn't into the thought of letting this woman flirt with him right in front of me.

He and Carina chatted a little more, and the woman paid no attention to me at all. It might have been tradition, but I didn't like being treated as though I was nothing more than arm candy. I knew Josh saw me as more than that, but still—did she really think I was just here because I happened to look good on his arm?

She arrived outside our room, smiling as she reached for the keys Josh was holding to slip them into the door. She made sure her fingers brushed against his. I stiffened again. I wanted to tell her I could see just what she was doing, but I knew there was no point. She would have just denied it. She finally glanced over at me, and I could see her lips set into a hard line, as though she wished I would just vanish already.

She pushed the door open for us, and led Josh inside, taking him by the arm and leaving me to follow. Did Josh even notice how she was acting? Maybe he was just waiting for her to go before he commented on it. But he had never been a man to hold back on speaking his mind. If he was pissed at the way she was acting, she would have known about it already, which said to me he didn't mind one little bit that she was treating me like this.

"If there's anything at all you need, Mr. Falcone," she remarked, leaning in close, close enough he could probably feel her breath, "you just let me know. Okay?"

"I will," he replied, and he glanced over and smiled at me as she headed out of the room at last.

"What's wrong?" he asked as she left.

I crossed my arms over my chest. "You really have to ask that?"

"I wouldn't be if I already knew," he replied, furrowing his brow. "What happened? Are you feeling okay?"

"I was until that girl start putting her hands on you," I muttered. He glanced to the door, where she had just left.

"Carina?"

"Yeah, how do you know her?"

"She used to work with my father back in New York," he replied. "She's the reason we got rooms here. She's just being friendly—"

"To you, maybe," I replied. "She barely even looked at me."

"She's just shy," he protested, and I rolled my eyes.

"Yeah, forgive me if I don't buy that," I replied. "She was all over you. She wanted to pretend like I didn't exist."

"It wasn't that bad," he protested, but he didn't seem to have it in him to argue. It was clear this woman had the hots for him. Maybe thought she could get an in to the family business if she played her cards right, and I was surprised he was acting so naïve. He was a smart guy, smarter than he was acting right now, and I didn't get why he was so blank to what I was telling him.

"Yeah, it was," I replied. "You were talking about marrying me less than an hour ago, but you don't have anything to say when a woman like that disrespects me right to my face?"

"She's an old friend—"

"Who wants to be way more than that," I replied, raising my eyebrows. "You really couldn't see it?"

"I think you should get some sleep," he told me, doing his best to keep his voice steady. I tried to pull myself together. I wasn't going to let this ruin our time here. Yes, I was pissed, but maybe he was right. It would have been better for us to talk this out in the morning once we'd had some time to think.

There were two beds in the small apartment space we were staying in, and I decided I wanted to sleep apart from him for tonight. Just tonight. We were both so tired, and it was clear we weren't seeing eye to eye. I would deal with this Carina shit in the morning. If she was even still there. The way she had been acting, I wouldn't be surprised if she tried to sneak into his room in the middle of the night.

Why didn't she go for Tommy? He was single, after all. She wouldn't have had to cause any trouble if she had gone after him, but she had decided to flirt with Josh right in front of me anyway. Maybe she was one of those women who got off on hitting on men in front of their wives and girlfriends to prove how hot she was and how she could have men in the palm of her hand in an instant.

I washed up and climbed into the soft, cushy bed, listening as Josh did the same with his. I felt a pang. Was I overreacting? I wasn't going to stamp down my feelings anymore, not after what had happened the last time I'd done it. I knew Josh really cared about me, but there was this awful feeling deep in my stomach as I tried to forget what I had allowed to happen right under my nose just a few months ago. And yeah, Carina was far from my best friend, but that just made it easier to see the game she was playing. I didn't have those stupid blinders on I'd had with Kimmy.

I pulled the covers up to my chin and gazed up at the ceiling. This was still going to be a good trip. Of course it would be. I wasn't going to let one random flash of jealousy get in the way of what I had been looking forward to for so long. Josh and I were going to work out what we would do next, what our lives were going to look like now we were officially together.

Once I'd gotten enough sleep to think straight, of course.

I tossed and turned a little, the interaction with Carina playing on my mind. Maybe I was just being paranoid. But she was acting like she had a right to my man, and there was no way I was going to just sit back, relax, and let it happen. Was this something I was going to have to get used to? Women who thought they had a chance with Josh if they flirted hard enough? I got it; his family was rich, and I supposed there were women out there who were only interested in money, but still...

Suddenly, a noise caught my attention. It sounded like a bed squeaking, and I shifted around in mine to make sure I wasn't the one causing the commotion. But a moment later, it came again, and I realized it was leaking through the wall next to my bed.

Tommy was staying beside us, and by the sounds of it, he had gotten lucky at the bar he'd gone to. I frowned, trying not to let myself get pulled into it. I could hear a woman moaning, her high-pitched pleasure cutting through the still air around me, as well as Tommy groaning too. I shifted in bed, turning over so I could pull the pillow over my head.

How was this fair? The first night I was here, and instead of spending my time fooling around with Josh in our gorgeous room, I was listening to his brother getting laid instead. This was bullshit.

But this would be the only night I was here I didn't have fun, I promised myself. No matter what Carina thought she could do to seduce my man away from me. She didn't stand a chance. He was totally committed to me, and there was no way I was going to let some random girl like her scare me off. I might have had the misfortune of being with some creep before who didn't respect me enough to stay faithful, but Josh was never going to do that to me.

I closed my eyes and tried to block out the sound as best I could. From here on out, I was just going to get some sleep, get over the jetlag, and get on with my life. And my amazing vacation with the man I loved.

Chapter Twenty

Josh

I WOKE EARLY THE NEXT morning to the sound of the sea lapping up on the beach. And when I reached over to the bed beside me and remembered why Amber wasn't there, I frowned.

I still didn't really get what she had been so upset about last night. Yeah, maybe Carina had been a little flirty with me, but it wasn't a big deal, was it? People flirted; it didn't have to mean anyone was trying to cause problems. It was just a little fun, that was all.

But she didn't seem to view it the same way. Was this some hangover from her last relationship? Because there was no way in fucking hell I was going to put up with being compared to that asshole. Yeah, I had my issues, but I had done everything I could to prove to her in the time we had been together how much I valued her, how much I cared about her. Wasn't it enough?

I climbed out of bed and went to grab some of my luggage, digging through it until I came across my running gear. I needed to blow off some steam and forget about this mess for a while. Maybe she was just jetlagged and paranoid.

I hoped so. When she got up, maybe she would be feeling better, ready to actually talk it out instead of jumping to the same conclusions she had been last night. It would be best if I avoided Carina for the time being. I hadn't expected her to be so friendly, but I figured she just wanted to keep Tommy and me on her good side. No doubt he'd had the same treatment from her when he'd gotten back from the bar last night—if he had been able to stand up straight, that was.

It was cool out on the beach, and the air washed over me as I began my run. I just wanted to get out of my head for a while. It was such whiplash, going from being so romantic with Amber on the beach to having her argue with me and insist on sleeping in separate beds later that night. I'd hoped we would be able to christen our new lodgings that first evening, but she clearly had other ideas.

Shit. Maybe it was just better to give her time to think. When she realized how crazy she was being, she would come to me and apologize, I was sure of it. She was just dealing with the remnants of being treated like shit by her ex, and even if I didn't deserve to get the sting, I was the one there to pick it up.

I had never given her reason to think I would have a wandering eye, had I? I felt like I had done all I could to convince her I was totally dedicated to her, even though she'd been through some shit. I hadn't even glanced in the direction of another woman as long as we had been together, never had a reason to. When she was around, everything else just vanished completely. How could it not? I adored her. I wanted to spend every second of my time with her, every chance I got.

I paused for a moment to catch my breath as I looked out over the sea in front of me. So huge, so all-enveloping, for a moment, it felt like all my problems just vanished.

Or it did until the moment I felt a sharp pain on the back of my head, and my vision went completely black. Before I felt my knees slam into the ground, one thought rushed through my mind—I wished Amber and I hadn't fought last night.

When I opened my eyes once more, it was so dim I could hardly make anything out. I tried to stand up, but my limbs were bound to a chair below me. I grunted with annoyance and tried to pull myself free, still not entirely registering how serious this situation was. What the fuck was going on?

I didn't know where I was. Still in Italy? Probably. My head was throbbing, pounding so hard I was having a hard time peering into the darkness. I was pretty sure I could hear people talking, but I couldn't make out anything that was being said. Who the fuck were they? And why had they brought me here?

I strained against the restraints again, trying to find enough space to get out, but there was no room for me. Whoever had done this, they knew what they were doing, and they weren't going to let go of me so easily.

My body ached, my mind rushing with questions. Who even knew we were here? My father hadn't spread it around that we were planning on coming to Italy, it was a chance for us to get out of the country under the radar of everyone who might usually have been looking for us. The only people who might have known we were coming here would have been our own family. Who had my father told? I wished I'd gotten a list from him, some way to make certain I was clear on what was going on.

But I had been too distracted with Amber, with what the two of us were going to do when we got out of America. And now, she had no idea where I was, probably thought I had walked out on her after what had happened the night before. My heart clenched at the thought. I knew I was in danger, but she was the only thing on my mind right now, the only thing I could think of. I wanted her to be safe, to be happy, and I knew she couldn't be if I had been dragged all the way out here.

Suddenly, someone emerged from the shadows—a man who stood a little shorter than me, with thick wrinkles around his eyes and his mouth. He was smiling, though it didn't seem genuine. I struggled against my bindings again, trying to get myself free, but I couldn't do anything but sit there and wait for him to close in on me.

"Josh," he greeted me calmly. His voice sounded almost friendly, or it would have, had he and his goons not snatched me off the beach to drag me here. I had no doubt he was working with a group, because he couldn't have brought me all the way down to this place by himself. He didn't look strong enough.

"Let me go," I told him, keeping my voice as calm as I could. I knew there was nothing to be gained from letting him see me freaking out. I needed to keep myself together. I needed to play this as calmly as I could, and I might get out with my life.

The man laughed—a mirthless laugh that filled the space around us, as though he couldn't imagine giving me a break for a moment.

"You really think I brought you all the way down here just to set you free?" he asked me, shaking his head with amusement. "No. You're staying with me, Josh. It's where you belong. For now, at least."

"Why?" I asked. The more information I had, the better my chances of getting out of here in one piece. I just needed to figure out what they wanted from me and give it to them. I didn't want to stick around any longer than I needed to. I wanted to get back to Amber, to prove to her I hadn't just walked away when things had gotten tough. This man had no idea of that, but if he ruined things with the woman I loved, he would have some serious answering to do.

"You don't recognize me?" he replied, spreading his hands wide and pausing before me. I looked him up and down and shook my head.

"Am I supposed to?"

"I thought your father would have done a better job making sure you knew your family," he remarked. "I'm Gianmarco. Your father's cousin."

I stared at him. I hadn't heard a thing about this. Was this the man I was supposed to be working with now I was here? Why had he turned this into some sort of kidnapping scheme?

"And what do you think you're going to get out of this?" I demanded. "You want money? Is that it?"

"Of course it is, Josh," he replied as he crouched down in front of me, looking into my eyes with a wide grin on his face. "Your father has been holding on to the family fortune for far too long. Don't you think it's time he shared it a little?"

"You're ransoming me?"

"Something like that," he replied, getting to his feet once more. He seemed utterly calm right now, as though there wasn't a thing in the world for him to worry about. It spooked me. He had clearly planned this down to the very last detail. He was utterly in control here, and he knew it. Nothing was going to throw him off his game.

"You should have taken Tommy," I told him. "You would have gotten more money for him. He's the one my father really wants to keep around."

He smirked. "Maybe," he replied. "But I get the feeling we're going to make good money off you, too. You're twins, aren't you? So basically the same anyway."

I bristled. I knew he was just trying to rile me up, but it was working. I hated it when people talked about us as though we might as well have been the very same person. We were different. More different than I would have cared to admit, actually.

And I knew Tommy would have been the one my father really cared about. Yes, he would get me back; I wasn't scared of him just leaving me here. But he would have handed over his entire fortune to get Tommy home safe and sound, and I wasn't sure the same could be said for me.

I sat back in the seat. If I was going to be stuck here for as long as they wanted to keep me, I could handle it. I would get out. I wasn't going to hurt myself.

"Well, I'll leave you to get settled in," he remarked, and he eyed me one last time, as though making sure I was really tied to the spot and not going anywhere. I almost wanted to dare him to untie me, let me fight it out with him, but I knew he would never have been so stupid.

He turned and walked out of the room I was being held in, and I listened as the door slid shut behind him. Shit. I was in trouble here. If I could find a way to get out, I would save my father the trouble of paying for me, and I knew it would put me in his good books.

But if I stayed caught, I was going to cost him. And if I cost him, I might just lose the goodwill I had managed to build with him so far.

And I didn't want to make all my hard work useless.

Chapter Twenty-One

Josh

I SPAT OUT A MOUTHFUL of blood and stared down the camera lens again. How many more times were they going to make me do this before they let me rest?

It had been about twenty-four hours since I'd been taken—at least, from what I could tell of the light leaking in through one of the broken windows not far from the chair I was being held in. People must have noticed I was missing by now, and I was sure they would have been looking for me. But how long were they going to make me wait to get out? I couldn't just sit around here and hope for the best. I needed help, and I needed it soon.

They had already gotten me to make one video for my father, begging him for the money they wanted for my release. I'd hated every second of it, but I didn't see a way out of it. The easier I made it on them, the less likely I was to get hurt—or at least, that's what I'd figured.

But when they'd come back a few hours later and told me they wanted me to make another one, I'd had something to say about it.

"Why the fuck would you need me to make a new one?" I demanded. "I just filmed a video for him. Can't you use that?"

"Listen," one of the men growled, getting right up in my face as he pulled off my bindings. "You'll do as we say. You get it?"

"And if I don't?" I replied. I knew I had at least a little leeway here. They needed me to play by their rules, and they would do anything they could to make sure I did. If I refused to go along with what they needed from me, they would be in trouble, since the last video I'd made clearly hadn't been enough for them to get what they wanted from my father.

The man yanked me to my feet and glowered at me as he stood there before me, looking me up and down.

"You don't want to know," he snarled back at me. I couldn't help but grin at him. I knew I was toeing a dangerous line, but I was stuck here, getting aggravated by how little I could do to change my situation, and I would be damned if I just sat around and let them dictate how things were going to be.

"I do," I replied. "I'm going to find out, I guess. Because I'm not filming that thing for you."

He grabbed me by the lapels and jammed his face into mine, so he was just an inch or two from me. I could smell his foul breath, and it took everything I had just to keep looking him in the eye and daring him to do something about it.

"You will," he warned me. "Remember who you're dealing with here."

"I have no fucking idea who you are," I replied, letting the smile spread a little wider over my face. "And I don't do anything for nobodies like you."

He swung for me then, and I supposed I deserved it. I hated feeling as though I had no control over a situation, and any way I could get it back, I would, even if it was as stupid as letting this fucker go for me because I had been winding him up since the moment he had stepped through the door. I tried to fight back a little, but another one of them pounced on me too, and before I knew it, I was on the ground covering my head and hoping they were going to be done soon.

Once they had made their point, they pulled me on to the chair and pointed the lens of the old video camera at me again. I stared down the black eye of the lens and tried to think about what I was supposed to say. I knew I was supposed to plead for my life, and with the blood dripping from my lower lip and the pain radiating through my face from where they had struck me, it wouldn't take much to convince anyone watching I was in a seriously bad way.

I managed to get out a few words, enough to satisfy them, and they headed off to do whatever they needed to do with the footage they had. I wondered how my father was responding to all of this, if he was worried or if there was a part of him that wanted to leave me here to deal with my own shit. If it had been Tommy, I knew he would have gotten him out already, but I didn't know where I stood on his list of priorities for the time being.

It bugged me. I knew we had been getting closer in the time before I'd left, but now that I was here, I wasn't sure how much of it I could rely on to come through. I wanted to believe he would be there for me, but how much could I expect, after I had let him down a million times over? He had laid his hands on me before, and maybe he thought I deserved this treatment for everything I had put him and the family through.

I wanted to believe he was kinder than that, but how could I know for sure? It wasn't as though I had any experience dealing with him in situations like this. I just wanted to get back to Amber, to assure her I hadn't left her after our fight the night before, and it was hard to stay focused on anything else.

I was worried about her. How would she be coping, in a new place like this, without me there to help her? I knew she was a strong woman, stronger than she would ever give herself credit for, but she had just been thrown into the deep end of everything I had wanted to keep away from her. I didn't want her to have to cope with this. I knew Tommy would be helping, but this would bring home to her how serious things could get. What if she didn't want to stick it out?

I didn't know how I would cope if she decided she was done with this. Maybe it would all be too much for her, the seriousness of all of this getting the better of her in ways she couldn't deal with. I knew she must have been struggling right now, and I prayed that Tommy was doing everything he could to show her she had nothing to worry about. I was going to be okay.

Well, as long as I could keep my fucking mouth shut, anyway.

Now I was tied back to the chair, I couldn't so much as wipe away the blood drooling from my mouth right now. The pain was intense, but it seemed distant as my mind raced on what I needed to do next.

I knew my father would have told me to keep my mouth shut, keep my head down, and just do whatever they asked of me so I could get out of this alive. And he would have been right, but I couldn't let it go so easily. There was a part of me that wanted to push back, to see how much they would take from me before they started to get tired of me. It was something I'd dealt with in a lot of my relationships, even the business ones, that feeling like I had to make it as hard as I could to see how much they would put up with.

But these guys would hurt me. They would cause me some serious fucking harm if I pushed my luck any further than I already had. I had to be careful, I had to play it cool, I had to control myself even though I wanted to test the boundaries.

And I wanted, more than anything, to get back to Amber. I needed to see her, to tell her everything was going to be okay. I prayed they wouldn't have gone after her, too. Given that this was about my father, I doubted it, but you could never tell with guys like this. Sometimes, they would go scatter-shot just to cause as much damage as they could, and I was scared Amber might have been caught up in the midst of it. I would never forgive myself if something happened to her, never.

I managed to doze off for a little while and when I came to, Gianmarco was standing over me once again, looking down at me with an expression of obvious disdain on his face. He didn't like me, probably didn't like having me around here one little bit. I hoped that meant he would let me go sooner rather than later, but I got the feeling he wouldn't have gone this far just to let it fail at the last moment.

"What do you want?" I snapped at him. I needed him to think I was ready to fight at any moment, ready to throw down no matter what it took.

"I want you to know where we stand," he replied, his voice as cool as it always had been. He wasn't giving away a single inch of emotion right now, not letting me see beneath the mask. He was in control here. All the other guys I had seen, they had nothing on his calm and collection.

"And where is that?" I asked. "You ready to let me go yet?"

He snorted with amusement. "Not yet," he replied. "We're still waiting on your father to send us the money we're owed."

I didn't know how much they were asking for from him, but I figured it must have been substantial. Something serious. They knew how much money my father had to his name, and they were going to exploit every penny of it as best they could now they had me here.

"I think we're going to give him another twenty-four hours or so," he continued, as he paced around my chair. "Do you think that sounds fair? Enough time for him to get everything together?"

I knew he wasn't really asking, and I didn't reply.

"I thought so," he continued. "So that's what I've given him. One more day. And after that...well, I think you should pray he sends the money along so you don't find out what we're planning for you next."

I stiffened. I had thought they were just going to keep me here as long as it took to get what they wanted from me, but clearly, they had a time limit in mind.

"Which is?" I asked, straining my aching neck around so I could look at him.

He leaned toward me and planted a finger in the middle of my forehead.

"A bullet," he told me. "Right here. One shot. And you won't know a thing about what comes next."

I shivered. I didn't want to show him I was scared. I forced a grin on to my face.

"Oh, that's it?" I asked, sounding as flippant as I could manage given the situation. "I thought you were talking about something way more serious."

He frowned, his eyes darkening with anger. He wanted me to be scared and cowering and begging him for my life, but he'd taken the wrong guy if he thought I was ever going to give him the satisfaction. He was an asshole, an asshole doing his very best to intimidate me and make me feel like there was no way out of this, when I knew better. I knew better than to believe him. He wanted me on edge, ready to beg and plead for my life, ready to do anything it took to get on his good side so I could survive a little longer. Tommy might have begged, but I never would.

Before I could say another word, he slammed his head into mine, and the world went black again.

Chapter Twenty-Two

Amber

I SAT ON THE EDGE OF the bed, feeling as though I was hanging twenty feet above the ground, trying to work out what the fuck I was meant to do next.

Josh was gone. It had been about five hours since we'd heard from his father, who had let us know he'd been contacted by some kidnappers demanding cash for his son's safe release. I couldn't believe this was happening, it was supposed to be our perfect trip away together, but instead—instead, it all seemed like it was falling apart even as I tried to handle the grinding pain of being away from him.

I hated that he had vanished right after we'd had an argument. I wished I could go back in time and get him to sleep in the same bed as me, tell him I didn't want him anywhere but right by my side, but it was too late for that now. He was gone. He was gone, and I had no idea who he was with or where he had been taken or what state he was in, and it was killing me.

Tommy was pacing back and forth in his room, talking to his father as they tried to work out what to do next. It seemed like the two of them were just trying to get through this without losing their minds, and I didn't blame them. If it was hard for me, the woman who loved him, how would it feel for the people who were his actual family? His mother must have been beside herself with worry, if his father had even said anything to her about this. I got the feeling he would keep it to himself if he got the chance, trying to make it so she didn't have to worry about everything when it was under his control.

Tommy had insisted I come to his room, wanting to keep an eye on me while everything was going down. He didn't want anything to happen to me, he had told me—that Josh would beat the shit out of him if I ended up hurt in all of this. I didn't want anyone to have to worry about me right now, but I figured it wasn't like I had much of a choice. Tommy wasn't going to let me out of his sight as long as he could, wanting to ensure I was okay and that he didn't have to worry about anyone else.

I could hear him on the phone to his father, but I couldn't take in anything of what he was saying. My mind was on Josh, on what he must have been going through right now. He would have been terrified, though there was no way he would have let anyone else see it. I wished I could be there with him, hold his hand, and promise him he had nothing to worry about, that his father would jump in and get him out of there the first chance he got.

But I didn't know if it was true. They were asking for a million dollars. It was a lot of money to move in a short period of time, and I knew his father was worried about getting it over there before the deadline. But there was no way he was going to fail, right? No way he was actually just going to leave his son out there to deal with all of this on his own. What would happen to Josh if his father didn't pay the money they were demanding? Would he die? Would they kill him? I could hardly even consider it, but I knew it was true. My heart was slamming against my chest as I tried to push the reality of it down inside my mind. I couldn't even consider losing him. I couldn't.

I would have sold everything he had bought for me if it was enough to pay to have him back. I would have done anything it took to make sure he was okay. I couldn't believe I had fought with him on the night before he had been taken. I would have done anything to turn back time and make it so he was there with me instead. I couldn't believe I had been so stupid, couldn't believe I had let him get so far from me. I needed him back. I needed him okay. I would have done anything to make sure it happened, but there was nothing I could do to help, and it was making me feel utterly and completely useless.

Tommy finally hung up the phone and turned back to me. I could see the dark rings under his eyes, making it clear he hadn't slept a wink. I wished there was something I could do to lift some of the weight off his shoulders, but all I could do was just sit here and hope for the best.

"What's happening?" I asked him, rising to my feet.

"They want me to drop off the money," he explained. "Dad's getting it wired over and handled, and I'm going to take it down to them to make the exchange for Josh."

I let out a sigh of relief. Okay, so they weren't going to leave him out there alone, that was something. I was still scared for him, but at least I knew his father wanted him back.

"Thank goodness," I muttered, rubbing my hand over my face. "Can I come with you? To make sure he gets out okay?"

"No way," Tommy replied. "I don't want them to know about you. The more you stay out of this, the better."

I knew he was right, but the thought of just sitting around here and waiting for something to happen was almost more than I could take. I forced myself to swallow heavily, reminding myself why he was doing this in the first place. It was to make sure Josh was okay, and if I put myself in the middle of it, I might cause more problems than they could deal with.

"Okay," I muttered, and I glanced up at Tommy. I immediately saw that he was shaking, and I went to take his hands.

"It's going to be all right, Tommy," I assured him, as best I could. I knew it wasn't like he could trust me, even really believe me with everything happening right now, but I prayed he would be able to see how much I meant this. I wanted him to know I was being honest right now, needed him to understand I trusted him. I trusted him with the man I loved, and I couldn't think of much more of a statement of my belief in him than that.

As soon as our hands touched, though, I felt something shift inside of me. I had been doing my best not to think about what had happened back at Josh's apartment before we'd left, but the moment we connected, all of my attempts to push it down just vanished.

"Thank you," he replied, and he looked down at me—really looked at me, his eyes lingering on mine for far longer than they needed to. He could feel it, too, he could feel the desire between us. All the tension of the last day was building up inside of us, impossible to ignore, impossible to deny.

He pulled me into his arms, and I sank against him gratefully. I just wanted the promise of someone to make it all a little better, just for a moment. Someone who could make me forget about everything going on. I was missing Josh so badly, and Tommy was the only person I had here. As twins, there were so many similarities between them that sometimes it felt like the lines of my want were starting to get blurred.

I wrapped my arms around him, and he leaned his face down into my neck. He inhaled deeply, holding me close, and I didn't want to let him go. I didn't want this moment to end. I just...I needed to get lost in him for a moment longer, for a second or two before I had to go back to the real world. I knew this was dangerous, maybe even crazy for me to so much as entertain the desire I had for him, but I couldn't stop it. I needed a distraction. The emotions were running so high right now that I couldn't focus on anything else, and all I wanted was the comfort of a man who knew what I was going through.

Before I knew it, I could feel his hardness starting to stir beneath his jeans. Oh shit, was this really happening? Was I supposed to stop it? I knew I should have pulled away and shut this down, but I didn't want to, not yet, not even a little bit. To feel his desire for me turned me on, even though I knew it was wrong and I should have known better.

He pulled back, and his eyes were soft, stuck on mine. I knew what he wanted, and I knew what I wanted, too. I wished I had the power to stop myself, but as he leaned down to plant his lips on mine, I knew it didn't matter.

As soon as he kissed me, I felt everything else fall away. I couldn't feel guilty anymore, because there was just the here and now, the impossible passion of his lips on mine, the way he tasted, the way he felt. I didn't want this to end. His body was strong; I raked my hands over his chest, feeling the muscle there. He was so like Josh in so many ways, and yet as he bit down on my lower lip, I couldn't help but notice how dissimilar they were from one another, too. How much separated them, as well as how much seemed to hold them together.

He grasped my face in his hands and kissed me greedily, as though he had been waiting for this for longer than he could remember. I kissed him back, hardly able to control myself. I wanted this, I wanted him, I wanted everything he could give me right now. The distraction, the freedom from what was running through my head, even though there was so much we should have been focused on.

Before I knew it, I was tugging at his clothes, pulling his shirt off over his head and tossing it aside. We should have been focused on something else entirely right now, but it seemed impossible to even think about it as our frantic hands, starved for one another, traversed our bodies. I had to stop, but the wrongness just made it all the more right, and I knew there was nothing I could do to slow myself down.

"Fuck," he moaned against my lips as he brushed my hair back from my neck, his fingers tracing down one side of my shoulder. He knew just what he was doing, just how to touch me, just how to show me how much he wanted me, and I could already feel myself giving in.

But before we could go any further, there was a knock at the door, and the two of us sprang apart so fast it was like someone had shot a bolt of lightning through us. What the hell were we doing? He grabbed for his shirt, not even able to look at me, and I lowered my eyes to the ground. The passion was still pulsing through me, but I needed to control myself. I couldn't let it get the better of me. I needed to slow down, to stop, to get myself in hand. That was my boyfriend's fucking brother, for shit's sake, and as much as I wanted to put it all down to stress, I knew there was more to it than that.

I couldn't have both of them. I just couldn't. I was being selfish, selfish and self-centered. How could I even think of being with someone else when the man I loved was trapped by people capable of who knew what? Thinking about what they would do to him if the money didn't come through wasn't exactly making me feel any better.

Tommy opened the door, and Carina was standing on the other side. I had hated her the first time I had seen her, but now, it was different. All of this was different. She was on our side now, here to do what she could to help us, and I knew I needed to be a little more grateful for her presence.

"Tommy, there's a call for you," she told him urgently, her voice low. I didn't know how much she had found out about what was going on with Josh, but she seemed to understand at least that this was serious. She glanced over at me, and I swiftly looked away, praying she didn't read anything into the look on my face right now. The last thing I needed was for her to bust me for making out with my boyfriend's brother when he was in danger.

To think, I'd had the nerve to turn around and accuse Josh of not standing up for our relationship. I was such a fucking hypocrite. I wanted to put it down to the stress I was going through right now, but I knew in my heart of hearts it would have been a lie. I had noticed the desire between us before, and as much as I wanted to pretend it wasn't there, I knew there was something going on.

Tommy hurried out of the room and left me sitting there on the edge of the bed, trying to wrap my head around what the hell had just happened. I had no idea what I was meant to do now, what I was supposed to think.

The spark between Tommy and I had been intense. Seriously intense. Even now, I could feel myself throbbing with want for him, needing him, craving the feeling of him kissing me again. Was it just the comfort of having someone around who could take care of me now it felt like everything was falling apart? Or was there more to it? More to it than I would ever have wanted to put into words?

I didn't know right now. But one thing I did know for certain was that we needed to get Josh out of the mess he was in. I couldn't go on without him. I couldn't survive much longer in this place without him by my side.

And if he got back—no, when he got back—I could figure out what the hell was going on inside my head and my body for the two brothers.

Chapter Twenty-Three

Josh

I GLANCED TO THE WINDOW, where the light was starting to fade outside. I didn't know how much longer I had left before they got rid of me, but I didn't much like my chances.

It was only a matter of time before the clock ticked down for good. Giancarlo had been pacing around most of the day, not saying a word to me as he peered down at his watch. He wanted that money, and I got the feeling he didn't have the stomach to kill me, even if he did talk a big game about it.

My father would get me out of this, right? Of course he would. He had to. I knew Tommy wouldn't allow him to just leave me here to die. Tommy cared for me, Tommy knew we were a team. And Amber—Amber wouldn't have let anything happen to me. I knew I could rely on them. If nobody else had my back, they did, and I needed to trust they would come through right now.

It was all on my father. He was the one with the money. If he decided he didn't want to put up with me anymore, I would be done for, end of. Maybe he saw this as a good thing, a chance to get rid of me without having to pull the trigger himself...

I was starting to get delusional with hunger and fear. I knew he didn't see me like that. My father might have been a harsh man, but he was a man who cared about his family above all else, even to his own detriment sometimes.

My mom wouldn't even know about it, I was sure of that. Dad would have done all he could to keep it from her. She didn't like to be involved in the heavy stuff, and right now, it didn't get any heavier than this. If she'd known I was in so much danger, she would have been hysterical, and Dad didn't like handling her when she was in that state.

How long did I have left? I was so tired I could hardly think straight. All I could focus on was getting out. I refused to even entertain the idea of being stuck here. My body was already cramped and tense from being stuck in this chair for so long, and I longed to stretch my legs, step on to the beach, and leave all this behind.

I knew there would be ramifications. Even if they really did hand me over after my dad paid up, this wouldn't just fall away with no follow-up. Something as big as this was bound to leave marks behind, even when we wanted to leave it in the past for good.

Suddenly, I heard footsteps, and my head snapped up to see Tommy walking into the room, holding a metal briefcase. His face was drawn, but as soon as his eyes locked on to mine, he seemed to relax.

"Josh," he muttered, and he went to make a beeline for me—but before he could get close, Giancarlo stepped out in front of him, blocking his path to make sure he didn't get near me without paying what he was owed.

"You have the money?" he asked, and Tommy nodded, thrusting the suitcase in his direction.

"It's here," he replied. "Count it if you need to. It's all ready for you."

I could feel my emotions starting to get the better of me, beginning to sweep through me at the sight of my brother. For a moment there, I had thought he wasn't going to make it. I had really thought he wasn't going to be here for me. But now, he was standing in front of me, paying up everything Giancarlo had demanded so I could go free. I was beyond grateful, my relief bringing tears to my eyes.

"Is Amber okay?" I asked him, and he nodded.

"She's fine," he replied as Giancarlo popped open the case and started to count the money he had been given. I breathed a sigh of relief. She had been all I had been able to think about since I was brought here. I was just glad she hadn't turned on me, thought this was something to do with the fight we'd had the night before I'd been taken.

"Thank goodness," I muttered, and I looked over at Giancarlo, wondering how much longer he was going to keep me here. I wanted to leave. I needed to leave. I was starving, aching, thirsty, and in serious need of several stiff drinks. Most of all, though, I wanted to pull Amber into my arms and show her how much I had missed her, how determined I was not to let some petty argument get in the way of things between us ever again.

"Untie him," Giancarlo ordered his men, and they finally made their way over to my chair and started to undo my bindings. I breathed a sigh of relief, turning my wrists to release them after I had been freed. For a moment there, I had never expected to get out of here alive, but it looked as though he was actually going to stick to his promise and let me go. I supposed there was no point fighting my father on all of this—if he had failed to hold up his end of the bargain, my father would have turned on him in an instant, if he hadn't already. And I knew he didn't want an enemy the size of Mario Falcone after him.

I rose to my feet, and Tommy pulled me into a hug. I squeezed him right back. I had never been so happy in my entire life to see my brother, never so relieved, and I knew he would have done everything he could to take care of my girl while I was away, too. He seemed intent on making sure Amber was okay as I did, and I was relieved I had him to rely on if something happened to me.

"Come on, let's get you out of here," he told me, looping an arm around my waist and allowing me to lean on him. Even though I had only been here a couple of days, my legs were already starting to get a little shaky from disuse, and I was glad I had him to rely on.

But before we could reach the door, Giancarlo stepped out in front of us again. He had an unreadable expression on his face, something odd, and Tommy paused for a moment, glaring at him.

"Deal's done," he reminded him. "There's nothing more for us to say to one another. Let us out. Now."

"We agreed to let your brother go," he replied, narrowing his eyes at Tommy. "I don't recall agreeing to anything to do with you."

And a moment later, his men pounced.

Tommy was too quick for them, pushing me toward the open door the split second before they grabbed him by the shoulders. He slipped out from underneath them and swung a punch at the one nearest to him, sending him flying to the floor. I was dazed, almost in shock from everything that had happened.

But I couldn't let them take Tommy. I couldn't fail him, not when he had come here to get me out. The least I could do was fight for my brother, the person who had my back in all of this, even when it was hard, even when it felt impossible.

I dived for the other man trying to grab Tommy, slamming into him hard enough to send him sprawling to the ground. Rounding on Giancarlo, I grabbed him by the lapels and rammed my face into his, making sure he could see the anger in my eyes, just how much I meant this.

"You try *anything* like this again," I warned him, "and I will kill you. You understand me?"

Giancarlo tried to pull himself loose, but I didn't let go. I wasn't going to give him an out until I had heard it from him directly, that he understood just what he had done, just how seriously I had taken it.

"Tell me," I ordered him. "Tell me you understand."

He nodded slowly, looking over to his guys, the ones we had sent crashing to the ground. He knew there wasn't a hope in hell we were going to give him an easy out right now. I was going to do everything I could to make sure he understood what we were dealing with here. If he tried anything, anything at all, after the mess he had made of my trip to Italy, I was going to finish him off, and I knew I would have my father's blessing to do it.

I let go of him and turned to Tommy, satisfied I had made my point. The adrenaline was starting to wear off, and I needed to eat, to sleep, to rest. To see Amber and make sure I hadn't scared her with my absence.

"Come on," I told him. "Let's get out of here."

He nodded and led me to the door. I leaned on him heavily once more, glad he was there to help me through this.

"You got me out," I muttered to him, and he nodded.

"You really think I would have left you there?" he asked.

"I didn't think you would," I replied. "But Dad..."

"Dad wouldn't let some two-bit thug take you out," he replied firmly, cutting me off before I could even reach the end of that thought. "He cares about you, Josh. I know you have a hard time believing it sometimes, but he does."

"Yeah, because he has a hard time showing it," I pointed out.

"He got you out," he reminded me. "Don't forget that. It's what matters, right?"

"Sure," I replied. I was just glad to be out of that dingy place, into somewhere a little brighter. I wasn't even sure where I was, but I figured I couldn't have been too far from the hotel, given they hadn't had a whole lot of time to move me.

The sense of freedom was huge and an enormous relief. I wasn't sure how much I had resigned myself to death, but a part of me had given up. I'd been sure my father wouldn't pay up that much to get me out. But now I was free again, it was like I had a whole new lease on life, and I didn't want to miss out on a single part of it.

Especially the parts that revolved around Amber.

"Where's Amber?" I asked. "Is she okay?"

"She's back at the hotel," he assured me. "And she's fine. Shaken, of course, and she's worried about you, but she's fine."

I nodded. I knew she was going to be freaked when she saw the wounds I was still carrying from where they had beaten me up, but she would be able to see I was okay underneath it. A little time to heal, and it would be like none of it had ever happened in the first place.

Suddenly, I noticed Tommy was carrying something in his other hand—in the rush as we'd gotten out of there, I had hardly been able to pay attention to it, but when I spotted it, I couldn't help but raise my eyebrows.

"Is that...?"

"The money they wanted for your ransom? Yeah," he replied, grinning. "I figured they broke the rules when they tried to take me. Dad'll be glad to have it back."

"You're not worried they're going to try and come after it again?"

"Not after what we did to them," he replied. "They're lucky we didn't take them out on the spot. He's going to leave us alone after this, money or no money."

I grinned. I should never have underestimated my brother. He always had my back, always looked out for our family, no matter what that meant. He would get that money back to my father, and all of this would be forgotten.

I felt a weight lift from my shoulders. It was all going to be okay. All of it. I just needed to keep my eyes forward and think about what came next.

Amber.

Chapter Twenty-Four

Josh

AS SOON AS I LAID EYES on her, I felt a wash of emotion get the better of me. She practically sprang into my arms, wrapping them around me and holding me close.

"Oh my goodness, Josh, you're alive," she blurted out, her voice edged with tears and desperation. I closed my eyes and buried my face into her neck, inhaling the scent of her and reminding myself how good it felt to be here with her again.

"I am," I murmured into her ear. "I was thinking about you the whole time. Are you okay?"

"I'm okay," she replied, pulling back and wiping away the tears from her face. She looked exhausted, even more so than I did, and I hated how worried she must have been this whole time. She didn't deserve to deal with this, she didn't deserve to be thrown into the deep end the way she had been. This was supposed to be a trip for the two of us to just spend some time together and blow off steam, but instead, we had wound up caught in a bigger mess than I could ever have imagined.

"What happened to your face?" she asked, looking at me carefully.

"I'm fine, don't worry about it," I told her as she reached up to gingerly touch the bruise over my right eye. I winced, and she furrowed her brow.

"Sorry, I didn't mean to hurt you..."

"It's okay," I promised her. "Really. I'll heal up fine."

"Did you deal with them? The guys who took you?" she asked. I glanced to Tommy, who was standing just behind her, and nodded.

"Yeah, they're not going to cause us any trouble again," I promised her. "But we should get out of here. I want to get back home already."

"Agreed," she sighed, and she leaned in to kiss me on the lips. I closed my eyes and let myself focus on nothing more but how good it felt to be here with her again. I'd been so scared I might not get a chance to do this, to touch her and hold her and kiss her, but I did. I had. Our stupid argument was all forgotten now, and, if anything, the kidnapping had just thrown into sharp relief how much I wanted her, how little anything else mattered right now.

Tommy was fiddling with the suitcase behind us, trying to give us some privacy. He had been kind of weird since I'd mentioned Amber, actually, as though he was bothered by her. Maybe he was just tired of dealing with her worry and concern in the time since I had been taken. I was sure she must have been frantic, and it couldn't have been easy for him to handle that on top of his own issues.

I clasped her face in my hands and looked deeply into her eyes, trying to remember every little detail of her. I never wanted to be apart from her again. Being separated had been more than I could bear, and I was just so relieved I'd gotten a chance to be here with her once more. I never wanted it to end. I wanted her here with me, every chance I got. I wanted her by my side. It was where she belonged.

"We can talk about the Carina stuff—"

"We don't need to," she assured me. "Honestly. Forget about it. I was overreacting. None of it matters anymore. It just matters that you're back here with me again."

She leaned her head against mine and closed her eyes, as though taking in the relief of having me there. It was almost impossible to remember what we had been fighting about in the first place. It didn't matter. We were together again, and everything else could wait.

When she pulled back, she glanced over at Tommy for a moment. I guessed the two of them must have gotten closer in the time since I had been taken; they wouldn't really have had much of a choice. They had been stuck together trying to navigate the mess of my kidnapping, supporting each other through the worst of it. I was just grateful Tommy had been able to look out for her this whole time, take care of her when she was going through it. She must have been so scared. She had never dealt with anything like this before.

We headed back to our room to start getting packed up. She had hardly even taken anything out of her suitcase, clearly too distracted with what had been happening. I could hardly even remember the fight we'd had before I'd been taken. I knew it had something to do with Carina, but it was all so blurred and distant now it didn't seem important. We could handle it later. I was pretty sure, after this, we were going to be able to handle anything the world threw at us.

She sat on the edge of the bed and watched as I filled up my suitcase with the few things I had taken out of it. She was chewing her lip hard, as though something was on her mind, and I glanced over at her.

"You okay?" I asked, and she blinked and nodded quickly.

"Oh, yeah, I'm good," she replied. "Just...glad you're back, that's all."

"Me too," I agreed. "Are you packed?"

"Pretty much," she replied, looking over to her bag. "I think I just have a few things left...shit, I think I left them next door. Give me a minute."

She slipped out of the room, leaving me to finish packing up on my own. I couldn't wait to get out of there, honestly. I had thought this trip would be a chance for me to get closer to Amber, for the two of us to make sure our relationship was as solid as it could be, but all that had happened was stress and danger, and I was done with it. I wanted to leave all this behind us, once and for all. And yeah, maybe it wasn't the romantic trip I had hoped to give her since she had just graduated, but I could make sure to shower her with all the attention and affection I could when we got home. I wanted her to know she had been on my mind the whole time I had been gone, that losing out on the life we had planned together had scared the shit out of me.

I wanted a future with her. I really did. When I had told her I could imagine marrying her, I had meant it with every fiber of my being. I wanted to make her my wife, I wanted her to be the mother of my children—I wanted her to be there for all of it, every little moment. In the dark and the pain and the confusion of being taken, she had been a light to cut through all of it, a promise of what was waiting for me on the other side when I got out.

Her and Tommy, of course. He was the one who had come to get me. No doubt he was the one who had put pressure on my father to free me, too. I wasn't sure I believed him when he said Dad had jumped at the chance to do it, but I wanted to. When I got back and saw my family again, I figured I would have a better idea of what had really happened there.

I couldn't believe how much I was looking forward to seeing him. I had been talking with Amber just a couple of days before about the possibility of getting out of this business, but if I hadn't been a part of it, I would have been stuck there for longer than I cared to even think about. If worse hadn't happened, of course.

But then, if I hadn't been my father's son, the chances they would have taken me at all would have been virtually nil. It came with pros and cons, and I needed time to weigh them inside my head, work out just what I wanted from this and if I could really get it.

I glanced over my bag and realized there were a few toiletries I still needed before we could hit the road. I wasn't sure if I had packed them, probably planning to pick them up while I was in Italy, but I would need them for the trip back. I was sure Tommy would have some to spare. He was always more sensible than me about this kind of thing.

I headed to his room, but when I opened the door, I was surprised to see it was empty. Amber had said she was coming here to grab some of her stuff, but I couldn't see her anywhere. A sneaking dread began to creep up the back of my spine. Had something happened to her? Had someone taken her...?

I made my way through the room, looking out on to the balcony, but there was nobody there, either. The suitcase with the money sat next to the bed, practically glowing with light, and I wondered how we were going to get it back to my father without raising suspicion.

I could figure that out later. For now, I was worried about Amber. And Tommy, for that matter. Where were they? What were they doing? Why couldn't I find them?

I heard a noise from the bathroom. It sounded like—it sounded like a moan. But there was no way—maybe Tommy had started something with one of the women who worked here. It was the only thing to explain it, but I was sure he wouldn't have allowed himself to get so distracted. I made my way to the door, hovering outside it for a moment, wondering if I should knock, before I reminded myself this was my brother. It wasn't like we had to be careful around each other.

I pushed the door open, and what I saw on the other side made my jaw hit the fucking floor.

Amber. Amber and Tommy, to be precise. She was on the bathroom counter, her legs wrapped around him, her hands in his hair. He was gripping her waist, kissing her hard, his body pushing against hers. They were still clothed, but it was clear neither of them wanted to be. I blinked, waiting for this to vanish in front of me, some invention of my over-tired mind.

But it didn't.

Amber sprang away from him, practically shoving him off her, but I had already seen it. Seen the two of them together, kissing, holding each other as though it was the most natural thing in the world. My brain was having a hard time processing what I had just seen, but there was no denying it. It had happened.

"Josh, I can explain," Tommy blurted out, but I didn't want to hear it from him. What the fuck could he possibly say to make any of this better? I knew betrayal when I saw it, when I felt it, and right now, it was screaming in my ears, so loud I couldn't think or feel anything else.

They were making out. Kissing. How long had this been going on? Before I had been taken? Had it started afterwards? A million questions were rushing through my mind, but I didn't even want the answers to any of them. I didn't want them to explain themselves to me; I could already see what they were doing, and I didn't need to ask what was happening. Whatever excuses they would have thrown at me, they would have been nothing more than attempts to shut me up, to get me to ignore what my intuition was screaming at me right now.

She had fucking betrayed me. They both had. The two people I was supposed to be able to trust more than anyone in the world, and they had betrayed me. As I stormed out of the bathroom, I could hear Amber calling to me, her hand on my shoulder, but I shrugged it off. If she thought I was going to let this slide—her making out with my damn *brother*—she had another think coming. She must have thought I was stupid. No wonder the two of them had been acting so strangely...

I needed to get out of here. I needed to put as much space between me and them as I possibly could. I couldn't stand to be anywhere near them right now. After everything I had gone through, everything that had happened, they did this to me? They fucked me around? They cheated on me?

I could feel my blood rushing in my ears, my body responding to the shock and horror with such distress that nothing else made sense. I had already been through enough, and now, this...

I wanted to get out. Put as much space between myself and those lying, cheating fucks as I could. The image of them together was already burned on the back of my eyeballs, and I wasn't sure I would ever get rid of it.

I snatched up the case as I rushed out of the room, not thinking straight. I needed to get out of there. I didn't care what damage it caused in the long run—everyone would take my side when they found out what the two of them had done. Those fucking pigs, going behind my back after I had been kidnapped...I had expected better of both of them, but I should have known the only person I could really trust was myself. Everyone else was a danger.

I slammed the door behind me and strode to the front door of the hotel. I wasn't giving them a chance to explain.

I didn't know what the Italian night would hold for me, but it was better than being stuck with them—the people who had turned their back on me, betrayed me, showed me they didn't give a single damn about me. I was out of here. Whatever I found waiting for me out there, at least it couldn't hurt me like they had.

THE END

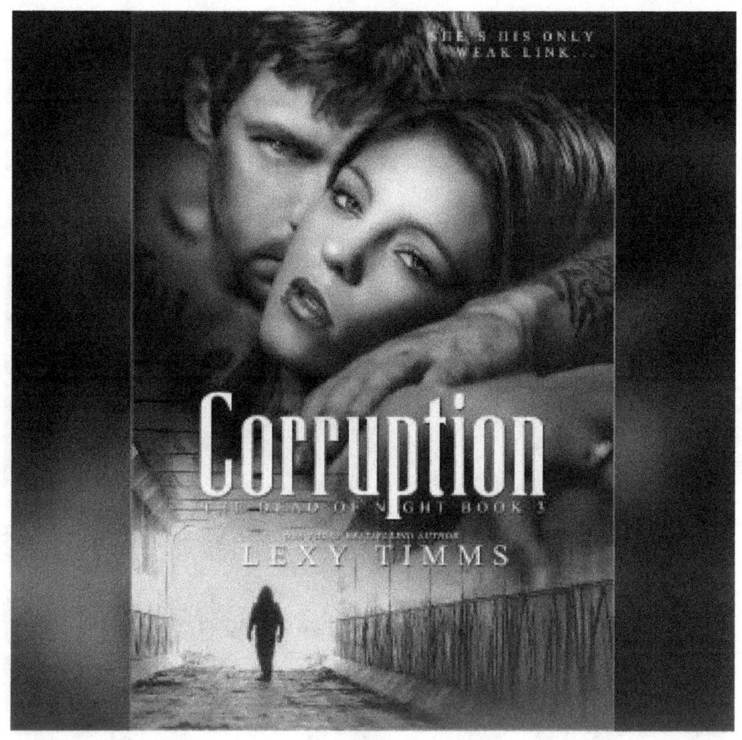
SHE'S HIS ONLY
WEAK LINK...
Corruption
LEXY TIMMS

The Dead of Night Series

Abduction
Bribery
Corruption

The Heat of Night Series

Depravity
Scandal
Disgrace

Find Lexy Timms:

LEXY TIMMS NEWSLETTER:

http://www.lexytimms/newsletter

Lexy Timms Facebook Page:

https://www.facebook.com/LexyTimmsAuthor

Lexy Timms Website:

http://www.lexytimms.com

BOSS
BOSS
BOSS
Lexy
Timms
Managing
BOSSES
Lexy
Timms
FREE
for a
Limited
Time

Want

FREE READS?

Sign up for Lexy Timms' newsletter
And she'll send you updates on new releases,
ARC copies of books and a whole lotta fun!

Sign up for news and updates!
http://www.lexytimms/newsletter

More by Lexy Timms:

FROM BEST SELLING AUTHOR, Lexy Timms, comes a billionaire romance that'll make you swoon and fall in love all over again.

Jamie Connors has given up on men. Despite being smart, pretty, and just slightly overweight, she's a magnet for the kind of guys that don't stay around.

Her sister's wedding is at the foreground of the family's attention. Jamie would be fine with it if her sister wasn't pressuring her to lose weight so she'll fit in the maid of honor dress, her mother would get off her case and her ex-boyfriend wasn't about to become her brother-in-law.

Determined to step out on her own, she accepts a PA position from billionaire Alex Reid. The job includes an apartment on his property and gets her out of living in her parent's basement.

Jamie must balance her life and somehow figure out how to manage her billionaire boss, without falling in love with him.

** The Boss is book 1 in the Managing the Bosses series. All your questions won't be answered in the first book. It may end on a cliff hanger.

For mature audiences only. There are adult situations, but this is a love story, NOT erotica.

THE ONE YOU CAN'T FORGET

Emily Rose Dougherty is a good Catholic girl from mythical Walkerville, CT. She had somehow managed to get herself into a heap trouble with the law, all because an ex-boyfriend has decided to make things difficult.

Luke "Spade" Wade owns a Motorcycle repair shop and is the Road Captain for Hades' Spawn MC. He's shocked when he reads in the paper that his old high school flame has been arrested. She's always been the one he couldn't forget.

Will destiny let them find each other again? Or what happens in the past, best left for the history books?

** *This is book 1 of the Hades' Spawn MC Series. All your questions may not be answered in the first book.*

Don't miss out!

Visit the website below and you can sign up to receive emails whenever Lexy Timms publishes a new book. There's no charge and no obligation.

https://books2read.com/r/B-A-NNL-DYUDC

Did you love *Bribery*? Then you should read *Taken By The Mob Boss*[1] by Lexy Timms!

[2]

EVIL begins when you start to treat people as things...

A kidnapping isn't how I expected to meet the woman of my dreams.

But when my brother, intent on proving himself as the hardcore gangster he wants to be, comes up with the idea to kidnap the daughter of a powerful crime boss, I know I can't stop him. And that's how I meet Charlotte.

Beautiful, intelligent, graceful – and hurting from the life she's been trapped into living. She wants to get out of this world just as much as I do, and it doesn't take long till we fall for each other, hard and fast.

Except time is running out for both of us.

---

1. https://books2read.com/u/3n7KMe
2. https://books2read.com/u/3n7KMe

If we're going to be together, we need to act fast – and do something that we can never renege on...

A DARK MAFIA ROMANCE SERIES

Book 1 – Taken By The Mob Boss

Book 2 – Truce With The Mob Boss

Book 3 – Taking Over The Mob Boss

Book 4 – Trouble For The Mob Boss

Book 5 – Tailored By The Mob Boss

Book 6 – Tricking By The Mob Boss

Read more at www.lexytimms.com.

Also by Lexy Timms

12 Days of Christmas
Snowflake Hollow - Part 1
Snowflake Hollow - Part 2
Snowflake Hollow - Part 3
Snowflake Hollow - Part 4
Snowflake Hollow - Part 5
Snowflake Hollow - Part 6
Snowflake Hollow - Part 7
Snowflake Hollow - Part 8
Snowflake Hollow - Part 9
Snowflake Hollow - Part 10
Snowflake Hollow - Part 11
Snowflake Hollow - Part 12
Snowflake Hollow - Complete Series

A Bad Boy Bullied Romance
I Hate You
I Hate You A Little Bit
I Hate You A Little Bit More

A Bump in the Road Series
Expecting Love
Selfless Act
Doctor's Orders

A Burning Love Series
Spark of Passion
Flame of Desire
Blaze of Ecstasy

A Chance at Forever Series
Forever Perfect
Forever Desired
Forever Together

A Dark Casino Romance Series
High Roller
Place Your Bet
All Or Nothing

A Dark Mafia Romance Series
Taken By The Mob Boss
Truce With The Mob Boss
Taking Over the Mob Boss

Trouble For The Mob Boss
Tailored By The Mob Boss
Tricking the Mob Boss

A Dating App Series
I've Been Matched
You've Been Matched
We've Been Matched

A "Kind of" Billionaire
Taking a Risk
Safety in Numbers
Pretend You're Mine

A Maybe Series
Maybe I Should
Maybe I Shouldn't
Maybe I Did

A Royal Affair Series
Royally F*cked
Royally Screwed
Royally Obsessed

Assisting the Boss Series

Billion Reasons
Duke of Delegation
Late Night Meetings
Delegating Love
Suitors and Admirers

BBW Romance Series
Capturing Her Beauty
Pursuing Her Dreams
Tracing Her Curves

Beating the Biker Series
Making Her His
Making the Break
Making of Them

Betrayal at the Bay Series
Devil's Bay
Devil's Deceit
Devil's Duplicity

Billionaire Banker Series
Banking on Him
Price of Passion
Investing in Love
Knowing Your Worth

Treasured Forever
Banking on Christmas
Billionaire Banker Box Set Books #1-3

Billionaire CEO Brothers
Tempting the Player
Late Night Boardroom
Reviewing the Perfomance
Result of Passion
Directing the Next Move
Touching the Assets

Billionaire Hitman Series
The Hit
The Job
The Run

Billionaire Holiday Romance Series
Driving Home for Christmas
The Valentine Getaway
Cruising Love
Billionaire Holiday Romance Box Set

Billionaire in Disguise Series
Facade
Illusion

Charade

Billionaire Secrets Series
The Secret
Freedom
Courage
Trust
Impulse
Billionaire Secrets Box Set Books #1-3

Blind Sight Series
See Me
Fix Me
Eyes On Me

Branded Series
Money or Nothing
What People Say
Give and Take

Building Billions
Building Billions - Part 1
Building Billions - Part 2
Building Billions - Part 3

Butler & Heiress Series
To Serve
For Duty
No Chore
All Wrapped Up

Change of Heart Series
The Heart Needs
The Heart Wants
The Heart Knows

Club Confession Series
Envy
Crave
Decoy
Urge
Oath
Club Confession Box Set Books #1-3

Cottage by the Sea Series
Surging Tide
Distant Shores
Twisting Ocean

Counting the Billions
Counting the Days
Counting On You
Counting the Kisses

Cry Wolf Reverse Harem Series
Beautiful & Wild
Misunderstood
Never Tamed

Dancing in the Cold Series
Cherry Picking

Darkest Night Series
Savage
Vicious
Brutal
Sinful
Fierce
Darkest Night Box Set Books 1-3

Dead of Night Series
Abduction
Bribery

Department of Defense Series
Dead Ahead
Blue Falcon
Joint Service
Indirect Attack

Devils MC Series
Pain
Ruin

Diamond in the Rough Anthology
Billionaire Rock
Billionaire Rock - part 2

Dirty Little Taboo Series
Flirting Touch
Denying Pleasure
Forbidding Desire
Craving Passion

Dominating PA Series
Her Personal Assistant - Part 1
Her Personal Assistant - Part 2
Her Personal Assistant Box Set

Fake Billionaire Series
Faking It
Temporary CEO
Caught in the Act
Never Tell A Lie
Fake Christmas
Fake Billionaire Box Set #1-3

Falling in Love Series
Small Town Charisma
Pleasing My Sweetheart
Switch My Future

Firehouse Romance Series
Caught in Flames
Burning With Desire
Craving the Heat
Firehouse Romance Complete Collection

Forging Billions Series
Dirty Money
Petty Cash
Payment Required

For His Pleasure
Elizabeth
Georgia
Madison

Fortune Riders MC Series
Billionaire Biker
Billionaire Ransom
Billionaire Misery
Fortune Riders Box Set - Books #1-3

Fragile Series
Fragile Touch
Fragile Kiss
Fragile Love

Great Temptation Series
The Devil's Footsteps
Heaven's Command
Mortals Surrender

Hades' Spawn Motorcycle Club
One You Can't Forget
One That Got Away

One That Came Back
One You Never Leave
One Christmas Night
Hades' Spawn MC Complete Series

Hard Rocked Series
Rhyme
Harmony
Lyrics

Heart of Stone Series
The Protector
The Guardian
The Warrior

Heart of the Battle Series
Celtic Viking
Celtic Rune
Celtic Mann
Heart of the Battle Series Box Set

Heistdom Series
Master Thief
Goldmine
Diamond Heist
Smile For Me

Your Move
Green With Envy
Saving Money

Highlander Wolf Series
Pack Run
Pack Land
Pack Rules

Hollyweird Fae Series
Inception of Gold
Disruption of Magic
Guardians of Twilight

How To Love A Spy
The Secret
The Secret Life
The Secret Wife

Just About Series
About Love
About Truth
About Forever
Just About Box Set Books #1-3

Justice Series
Seeking Justice
Finding Justice
Chasing Justice
Pursuing Justice
Justice - Complete Series

Karma Series
Walk Away
Make Him Pay
Perfect Revenge

King of Hades MC Series
Sinner
Tempting Sinner
Enticing Sinner

Kissed by Billions
Kissed by Passion
Kissed by Desire
Kissed by Love

Leaning Towards Trouble
Trouble

Discord
Tenacity

Love on the Sea Series
Ships Ahoy
Rough Sea
High Tide

Lovers in London Series
Risking Millions
Venture Capital
Worth the Expense
The Price of Luxury
Exclusive Passion
Sparkling Christmas
Lovers in London - 3 Book Box Set

Love You Series
Love Life
Need Love
My Love

Managing the Billionaire
Never Enough
Worth the Cost
Secret Admirers

Chasing Affection
Pressing Romance
Timeless Memories
Managing the Billionaire Box Set Books #1-3

Managing the Bosses Series
The Boss
The Boss Too
Who's the Boss Now
Love the Boss
I Do the Boss
Wife to the Boss
Employed by the Boss
Brother to the Boss
Senior Advisor to the Boss
Forever the Boss
Christmas With the Boss
Billionaire in Control
Billionaire Makes Millions
Billionaire at Work
Precious Little Thing
Priceless Love
Valentine Love
The Cost of Freedom
Trick or Treat
The Night Before Christmas
Gift for the Boss - Novella 3.5
Managing the Bosses Box Set #1-3
Managing the Bosses Novellas

Mislead by the Bad Boy Series
Deceived
Provoked
Betrayed

Model Mayhem Series
Shameless
Modesty
Imperfection

Moment in Time
Highlander's Bride
Victorian Bride
Modern Day Bride
A Royal Bride
Forever the Bride

Mountain Millionaire Series
Close to the Ridge
Crossing the Bluff
Climbing the Mount

My Best Friend's Sister
Hometown Calling

A Perfect Moment
Thrown in Together

My Darker Side Series
Darkest Hour
Time to Stop
Against the Light

Neverending Dream Series
Neverending Dream - Part 1
Neverending Dream - Part 2
Neverending Dream - Part 3
Neverending Dream - Part 4
Neverending Dream - Part 5
Neverending Dream Box Set Books #1-3

Outside the Octagon
Submit
Fight
Knockout

Protecting Diana Series
Her Bodyguard
Her Defender
Her Champion
Her Protector

Her Forever
Protecting Diana Box Set Books #1-3

Protecting Layla Series
His Mission
His Objective
His Devotion

Racing Hearts Series
Rush
Pace
Fast

Regency Romance Series
The Duchess Scandal - Part 1
The Duchess Scandal - Part 2

Reverse Harem Series
Primals
Archaic
Unitary

Roommate Wanted Series
The Roommate
The Bunkmate

The Flatmate

R&S Rich and Single Series

Alex Reid

Parker

Sebastian

Zane

Saving Forever

Saving Forever - Part 1

Saving Forever - Part 2

Saving Forever - Part 3

Saving Forever - Part 4

Saving Forever - Part 5

Saving Forever - Part 6

Saving Forever Part 7

Saving Forever - Part 8

Saving Forever Boxset Books #1-3

Secrets & Lies Series

Strange Secrets

Evading Secrets

Inspiring Secrets

Lies and Secrets

Mastering Secrets

Alluring Secrets

Secrets & Lies Box Set Books #1-3

Shifting Desires Series
Jungle Heat
Jungle Fever
Jungle Blaze

Sin Series
Payment for Sin
Atonement Within
Declaration of Love

Sins of the Father Series
The Betrayer

Southern Romance Series
Little Love Affair
Siege of the Heart
Freedom Forever
Soldier's Fortune

Spanked Series
Passion
Playmate
Pleasure

Spelling Love Series
The Author
The Book Boyfriend
The Words of Love

Strength & Style
Suits You, Sir
Tailor Made
Perfect Gentleman

Taboo Wedding Series
He Loves Me Not
With This Ring
Happily Ever After

Tattooist Series
Confession of a Tattooist
Surrender of a Tattooist
Heart of a Tattooist
Hopes & Dreams of a Tattooist

Tennessee Romance
Whisky Lullaby
Whisky Melody

Whisky Harmony

The Bad Boy Alpha Club

Battle Lines - Part 1

Battle Lines

The Brush Of Love Series

Every Night

Every Day

Every Time

Every Way

Every Touch

The Brush of Love Series Box Set Books #1-3

The City of Mayhem Series

True Mayhem

Relentless Chaos

Broken Disorder

The Coffee Shop Romance Series

A Rich Aftertaste

A Bitter Flavor

Baked to Perfection

The Debt

The Debt: Part 1 - Damn Horse
The Debt: Complete Collection

The Fire Inside Series
Dare Me
Defy Me
Burn Me

The Gentleman's Club Series
Gambler
Player
Wager

The Golden Game
On The Pitch
Respect the Game
All Game
Sweat and Tears
The Final Score
The Golden Game Box Set Books #1-3

The Golden Mail
Hot Off the Press
Extra! Extra!
Read All About It
Stop the Press

Breaking News
This Just In
The Golden Mail Box Set Books #1-3

The Long Con Series
The Misfit
The Hustle
The Cheat

The Lucky Billionaire Series
Lucky Break
Streak of Luck
Lucky in Love

The Millionaire's Pretty Woman Series
Perfect Stranger
Captive Devotion
Sweet Temptations

The Sound of Breaking Hearts Series
Disruption
Destroy
Devoted

The Takeover Series

Love Notes
Fine Print

The University of Gatica Series
The Recruiting Trip
Faster
Higher
Stronger
Dominate
No Rush
University of Gatica - The Complete Series

The Wrong Side of the Tracks
The Knockback
The Overshare
The Fightback

Timing is Everything Series
Right Time
Right Place
Right Reasons

T.N.T. Series
Troubled Nate Thomas - Part 1
Troubled Nate Thomas - Part 2
Troubled Nate Thomas - Part 3

Toxic Touch Series

Noxious

Lethal

Willful

Tainted

Craved

Toxic Touch Box Set Books #1-3

Undercover Boss Series

Marketing

Finance

Legal

Undercover Series

Perfect For Me

Perfect For You

Perfect For Us

Unknown Identity Series

Unknown

Unpublished

Unexposed

Unsure

Unwritten

Unknown Identity Box Set: Books #1-3

Unlucky Series
Unlucky in Love
UnWanted
UnLoved Forever

War Torn Letters Series
My Sweetheart
My Darling
My Beloved

Wet & Wild Series
Stormy Love
Savage Love
Secure Love

Worth It Series
Worth Billions
Worth Every Cent
Worth More Than Money

You & Me - A Bad Boy Romance
Just Me
Touch Me
Kiss Me

Standalone

Wash

Loving Charity

Summer Lovin'

Love & College

Billionaire Heart

First Love

Frisky and Fun Romance Box Collection

Beating Hades' Bikers

Everyone Loves a Bad Boy

Dead of Night

Christmas Countdown - The Advent Calendar

Watch for more at www.lexytimms.com.

About the Author

"Love should be something that lasts forever, not is lost forever." Visit USA TODAY BESTSELLING AUTHOR, LEXY TIMMS https://www.facebook.com/SavingForever *Please feel free to connect with me and share your comments. I love connecting with my readers.* Sign up for news and updates and freebies - I like spoiling my readers! http://eepurl.com/9i0vD website: www.lexytimms.com Dealing in Antique Jewelry and hanging out with her awesome hubby and three kids, Lexy Timms loves writing in her free time. MANAGING THE BOSSES is a bestselling 10-part series dipping into the lives of Alex Reid and Jamie Connors. Can a secretary really fall for her billionaire boss?

Read more at www.lexytimms.com.

About the Author

www.ingramcontent.com/pod-product-compliance
Lightning Source LLC
LaVergne TN
LVHW010550160826
845677LV00013B/3068

* 9 7 9 8 3 7 0 7 1 2 6 6 1 *